PUMPKINS AND PROMISES

HOLIDAY BEACH SWEET ROMANCES

ELLE RUSH

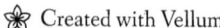

BLURB

Working full-time, going back to school, and raising a high school senior, Brooke Portman's schedule in Holiday Beach is a whirlwind of obligations. As she turns the page into October, the few blank spots left on her calendar are filled with the lawman who's determined that she should have a life with him in the picture.

Sheriff Aaron Gillespie thinks he and Brooke can go the distance. They just have to get past all the obstacles that the Halloween season throws in their path. Spooky sightings and mysterious disappearances keep interrupting the few moments he can steal away with Brooke.

All the false alarms and mischievous pranks have stretched the sheriff to the limit. A case of arson pushes him over the edge. Especially when it looks like Brooke is hiding something about his prime suspect. He'll need to either pull out his handcuffs, or set aside his badge and trust her. Either way, their relationship could be over before he can say, "Trick or treat."

CHAPTER 1

BROOKE PORTMAN BELTED out the last few bars of "Miss Independent" with a lot of energy and not a little amount of talent. She rarely attended karaoke night at the Escape Room, but tonight was a special occasion. It was the Monday evening of September's Labor Day weekend, and she was seeing it off with a bang. The tourists who had taken over her Minnesota resort town for the last three months had packed up and returned to their lives. Now the summer rush was over, and regular life was returning for the full-time residents of Holiday Beach. For Brooke, that meant her daughter would be home and starting her first day of her senior year of high school, and she would be restarting adult classes at the local community college.

If this was her last homework-free Monday for the four months, she was going to make it memorable. Which is why she was at a bar on Margarita Monday, grooving to Kelly Clarkson and earning an ear-splitting round of applause.

"Why haven't you been here before?" Lucy Callahan

demanded. Her palms were red from clapping so hard. "I've been coming here all spring and summer, and you haven't shown your face, let alone approached the microphone."

"My online lectures were on Monday nights. I couldn't afford to miss one."

"Okay, fine, that's a good reason," her friend relented. As she should, considering it had been Lucy who'd encouraged her to enroll for the online program in the first place. "All your hard work obviously paid off, Miss 4.0. Congratulations on your first college credit."

"One down, seven to go." It was hard going back almost twenty years after high school, but it had been necessary. Brooke had almost lost her job as head house-keeper at the Dew Drop Inn when it changed owners the previous spring. Her unstable future had stared her right in the face, and it wasn't a pretty sight. She decided then and there to work towards a better future for her and her daughter.

Roy Wagner, the bartender and bar owner, appeared beside them and wrapped his arm around Lucy's waist. "How are my two favorite customers?" he asked.

"I'm waiting for Brooke to do her encore," Lucy said as she leaned into him.

Brooke would have liked to stay longer, but she reached for her purse. "I can't tonight. I have to get home. Jordan is coming back tomorrow, and school starts the day after."

"How long has she been away?" Roy asked.

"Forever," was Brooke's quick answer. "Two months, since school ended. She spent the summer with her dad visiting his family in New Orleans." She'd missed her seventeen-year-old daughter like crazy. The two of them were as close as a mom and teenager could be. Letting Jordan spend the summer with her grandparents had been the right thing to do, but it hadn't been an easy decision.

"Then you should get one more song in before she gets back. I know Aaron is looking for a duet partner," Roy said. He lifted his hand and waved at a person behind them.

Lucy hopped off her bar stool. "I need another margarita. I'll be back."

"Don't you dare leave me!" It came out louder than the whisper she'd intended, but the music covered her slip. Aaron had been finding reasons to spend time with her for the last few months. He'd asked Brooke if she'd help organize the community's spring baseball schedule, and if she'd planned to chaperone any of the school dances. For the last couple months, every time Brooke turned around, he was there, smiling at her.

Lucy knew this. Still, all her friend did was raise her eyebrows and grin. "Later," she said, running off before Brooke could stop her. Aaron was suddenly in front of her and Roy.

"The Karaoke Queen and the Karaoke King together at last. When can we expect a duet?" Roy asked with an infuriating smile.

"I didn't know you did karaoke, Aaron."

"I'm nowhere as good as you. It is a good way to blow off some steam though." The handsome, sandy-haired man turned his back to her for a second and wagged a finger in Roy's face. "Forget it. Don't ask me to sing 'I Fought the Law' again."

"But Brooke would harmonize so well with you," the

bar owner protested. "Brooke, talk him into it. I have to make my girlfriend's drink."

Aaron slipped into Lucy's empty seat. "It wasn't funny the first time he asked."

Considering that Aaron Gillespie was the sheriff for Holiday Beach and the surrounding area, Brooke had to disagree. "It was a little funny."

Aaron gave her a wry grin, his hazel eyes laughing. "It's better than when he asks me to sing the *Cops* theme song."

She snorted into her margarita glass. "How's Trevor?" Aaron's son was the same age and in the same grade as her daughter, but they weren't really in the same social circles.

"Driving me nuts. It's like he gets paid a bonus every time he gets my blood pressure into the red zone."

"What's he doing now?"

"Nothing. That's what's so suspicious. He's been a model son for the last month. I'm waiting for the other shoe to drop."

"Maybe he's turned a corner," she suggested, although she didn't believe it herself. Jordan was a good kid too, but Brooke knew from experience that anything more than five days in a row of good behavior meant something was coming, be it bad news or a request for expensive concert tickets in Minneapolis. They were teenagers, after all.

"We'll see. He's promised to get himself organized for school on Wednesday, so I can guarantee I'm taking a quick late-night trip to the store tomorrow to buy all the things he's forgotten."

"Count yourself lucky. I had to promise to hold off till Jordan got home so she could approve all her new stuff, down to the pens. We're going to be shopping for hours."

She'd booked the day off as a vacation day for precisely that reason. Brooke was grateful Lucy had volunteered to cover her hours, even though Lucy wasn't technically a housekeeper. She was more of a Jill-of-all-trades for the hotel, and thankfully some of her skills included cleaning up after guests.

As the current singer wound down a rough version of "Living on a Prayer," Aaron applauded politely. "Roy was right about one thing. I am looking for a duet partner. Want to give it a go with me?"

Brooke froze. His interest was so confounding she could barely keep up her half of a conversation. In the spring, he'd started saying hello when he ran into her at the store or popping into the hotel and asking her how things were going when she was working. Aaron was always polite and funny and interested. But he never once took it a step beyond that, no matter how friendly she was in return. Now he was asking her to do a duet? She had no idea what he was up to. But her curiosity, and her desire to give him one last opportunity to make a move, overrode her common sense. "What were you thinking of singing?"

"Don't Stop Believin'."

His suggestion made her little musical-loving heart swooned. "Sure."

They were halfway through the first chorus when Brooke realized what she'd done. There was no way that performing with him was anything other than a signal to continue his half-hearted flirting. She gave herself a mental shake. Half-hearted attention was more than she'd received in months, even if she did wish that it was the real thing. As a single parent with a teenager, her dating life hadn't been anything to write home about since her divorce. Besides, Aaron never seemed to take it too seriously anyway, to her disappointment. She hadn't even received an invitation for a cup of coffee from him in all these months of conversation.

The revelation that she'd have to put up with her frustration for a while longer caused her to stumble over her next line, but she quickly glanced at the little bouncing ball on the screen and finished her verse. Another chorus, and they were done.

"We're not going to top that performance tonight, folks," Roy announced. "I declare Aaron and Brooke the champions to beat in October. We'll see you on the first Monday of October for the Escape Room's next karaoke night."

Aaron's smile was grateful when he looked at her. "Thanks for the duet. It was a lot of fun."

Despite her earlier misgivings, she had to agree. "It was."

"Maybe we can do it again sometime." But instead of waiting for an answer, he simply waved goodbye to Roy and left.

Lucy returned into her now empty seat. "Well?" she demanded. "How did it go? He's cute, *and* he's single. Any sparks? Because it looked like there was sparks. Did he finally ask you out?"

Brooke opened her mouth to speak then snapped it shut. "Cute" didn't describe Aaron Gillespie. He was tall and lanky and fit. He wasn't shaped like a bodybuilder, but he was too active to have a dad bod. He had great eyes and a slightly crooked smile. She tried again and still couldn't find the words for the mass of contradictions that was her duet partner. Finally, she spit out a single syllable. "Men!" she exclaimed.

"I'll take that as a no, then," Lucy said with a sigh.

"What is wrong with him? Is he being friendly? Because that wasn't a song for just friends to sing. Does he want to ask me out? I don't think I'm his type because he chases down bad guys for a living, and I'm not nearly that exciting. Is he messing with me? If so, it's working. But I have a job, a teenager, and night school. If he wants my attention, he's going to have to do a lot better than he has been." Brooke wasn't against the idea of dating, but the lucky fellow she decided on would have to make it worth her while. So far, Aaron wasn't measuring up.

Her outburst must have been louder than she'd realized. Lucy stared at her with wide blue eyes. Behind the bar, Roy's brown ones were equally big. "We'll let him know."

"No, don't!" She didn't need them interfering in her non-existent love life.

"That's what friends are for," Lucy insisted with a grin.

CHAPTER 2

AARON PULLED into the driveway of his four-bedroom bungalow, feeling good and relaxed for the first time in as long as he could remember. Tonight, he hadn't been on duty or on call, and it had been weeks since that had happened. An evening with good friends, good food, and good music was just what he needed. His duet with Brooke Portman was simply the cherry on top.

His grin turned to a grimace when he saw all the lights still on. It was after eleven. Trevor was supposed to have been in bed half an hour ago in anticipation of having some kind of normal sleep schedule when school started. For a brief second, he thought he'd get lucky and find his seventeen-year-old son asleep on the sofa. Then he walked from the garage, through the mudroom, and into the kitchen, and bellowed.

"Trevor!"

A black hole had formed in his kitchen. It didn't pull all the food in the fridge and cupboards into his son's stomach like it usually did. Instead, it had pulled every plate, casserole dish, box of cereal, and pan from every drawer, cupboard, and pantry shelf, and spread them across all the flat surfaces: table, counter, island, and floor. "What is going on here?" Aaron asked his son.

"It's okay, Dad. I have it all under control." His son's spiky chestnut hair, its color so similar to his mother's, was slicked back and dotted with dust.

"That doesn't answer my question, Trev. What are you doing?" This went beyond leaving a mess after making a sandwich before bed. The room was destroyed.

"It's our fall housecleaning." The teenager stuffed the last bite of a sandwich into his mouth and dropped the plate in the sink. "It started off with me making a snack, but the honey Dijon mustard had a clump of mold in it. I checked the bottle's best-before date, and it was in March. Then I found a jar of relish and two small, half-used bottles of expired mayonnaise in the back of the fridge from that Fourth of July barbecue we had two years ago. I pulled out the garbage can and went to town. See?"

Aaron was so shocked by the proud look on Trevor's face that it took him a moment to look past the open fridge door. The glass shelves gleamed under the bright white light; the fact he could see them at all was amazing. Jars were grouped by ingredients, meaning he could reach for pickles and not come out with spaghetti sauce. There was half a shelf of hot sauces and mustards, but they were together. Trevor pulled on a crisper drawer to reveal small containers separating apples from grapes and potatoes from onions.

Then Aaron noticed the overflowing garbage can on the counter, with a brown head of lettuce peeking out of the top. Jar-shaped bulges strained the plastic at the bottom.

"I don't think our fridge has looked that organized

since we brought it into the house empty," he praised. "But what about the rest of—" He waved his hands, indicating the rest of the mess.

"Well, then I looked in the pantry because I wanted some ravioli too. Since I was checking dates, I started looking at the cans and stuff. Dad, we had six-year-old pancake mix! Gross. And four cans of coconut milk." He raised a can of cola and took a swig. "That box," he said, pointing, "has stuff we won't eat that'll be expiring in the next four months. I figure we can donate it." He tossed his empty can into a recycling bin. "The other box is expired stuff that can probably still be used."

Aaron took the initiative and opened the door to their seldom-used walk-in pantry. Again, the shelves were spotless, organized, and half empty now that all the nearly empty cracker boxes and tortilla bags with three chips left were gone. "Very nice."

When he took a second look at the mess around the kitchen, he realized it was less a mess and more organized chaos, with bags and boxes and piles. "And the cupboards?"

Trevor shrugged. "At that point, I figured I might as well finish doing the kitchen, so I pulled out all the dishes. Then I ran out of energy and needed a snack."

Aaron rolled his shoulders. The last thing he wanted to do at eleven at night was reorganize the kitchen. His son may have inherited his mother's looks, but he got his father's procrastination habit. If they didn't finish tonight, they'd live like this for another month. But Aaron wasn't about to discourage future cleaning sprees. "Let's get this finished so we can enjoy fall with an amazing kitchen," he said. He rolled up the sleeves on his shirt. "We'll do the plates and glasses first. Then we'll tackle the rest."

Trevor didn't move quickly, but he did move. Soon their cupboards and drawers were filled with nested mixing bowls and properly stacked casserole dishes and lids. Aaron got into the swing of things and tossed out two frying pans with peeling Teflon that should have been thrown away years ago. They were left with a few odd pieces, some cracked mugs and chipped glasses, and enough yogurt and sour cream containers to stock a small dairy.

It was also close to midnight. "We'll deal with the recycling in the morning. Good job tonight, Trev. Really good," Aaron said.

After all the lights were out, Aaron listened to the silence. The two of them rattled around in the sprawling ranch house. Trevor basically had his own bathroom, since the other two bedrooms were staged as a never-used office and an often-used guest room. His own primary suite and equally huge, attached bathroom allowed him space to decompress after he took off his uniform.

Home, in general, wasn't always the most relaxing place to be. But every now and then, his son surprised him in a good way. The first few years of teenagerhood had been rough, with Trevor rebelling any way he could. Aaron and Tara divorcing at the same time hadn't helped. Lately, though, his son had been having more good days than bad. It was starting to feel like they were over the hump.

Aaron didn't think Trevor was doing well enough to bring a new variable into play though, which was why his interactions with Brooke Portman hadn't gone beyond flirting, despite his interest.

But he still looked forward to more karaoke nights with the pretty blonde.

CHAPTER 3

BROOKE JUMPED at the early morning knock on her apartment door. She was already awake; her mornings usually began at the crack of dawn as she cleaned the rooms of departing guests and prepared for new ones. But she felt guilty getting caught sitting on the sofa with a cup of coffee at seven in the morning on her day off.

Lucy's shining face greeted her. "Good morning. Here," her friend said, shoving a paper bag at her. "It's a welcome home present for Jordan. You said she's coming back today, right?"

Finding Lucy at her door was nothing new. When they'd first met, Lucy was doing property maintenance at the hotel where Brooke worked, but Lucy had since left to take a new job managing Brooke's apartment block complex. She'd whipped both properties into shape in no time. Seeing her this morning was a nice surprise. "Yes, today. She and Denny flew into Minneapolis late last night. They should be on the road now. This afternoon, we're buying everything on her back-to-school list."

"Do you have a second for a question right now?"

Brooke stepped aside to let her in. Lucy had already seen her place at its worst when a plumbing emergency turned her bathroom into a pond. A basket of laundry on the loveseat was nothing compared to that. It only took her a second to toss it into one of the apartment's two tiny bedrooms. "What's up?"

"It's more what isn't up. What do you know about the tenants in suite one-oh-four in Building B?" Lucy asked.

Brooke and Jordan had lived in their current complex for four years. With Holiday Beach as small as it was, there hadn't been much turnover in the renters in the three buildings. "That's the Quentins, isn't it?"

"It should be, according to the lease."

"Why? What's wrong?"

"I haven't seen either Mr. or Mrs. Quentin all summer."

Brooke knew all the tenants, at least by sight if she didn't speak to them regularly. When she stopped to think about it, she hadn't seen them lately either. "Neither have I, but I've seen their son Caleb around. Is something wrong?"

"No. I've been getting money orders in the manager's drop box to cover the rent. Their lease is up for renewal next month, and I'm trying to get a hold of them to sign the contract. It's not urgent. We still have time." Before Lucy could say anything else, an alarm on her phone sounded. "That was my last warning to get on the road to cover for a certain friend at the Dew Drop Inn."

"And your friend appreciates it. Although you can't tell me that you aren't going to sneak off for lunch with Roy since he'll be right next door."

"I will not sneak over to the bar," Lucy protested. Then she grinned. "He's bringing lunch to the hotel."

"Be gone with you, then, and let me enjoy my coffee." As she shooed her friend out of her apartment, she added, "I'm sure Jordan will come say hi tonight once she's home and settled."

"Sounds good. I'll get out of your hair for now, but if she wants to put on a back-to-school fashion show, I'm free."

Lucy's parting comments sent her scurrying into the small galley kitchen where her grocery list hung on the wall. She quickly added "Conditioner/oil/hair stuff" to the bottom of the sheet, then added a bunch of question marks. She hoped Denny's family had taken Jordan shopping in New Orleans; beauty products for Black hair were hard to come by in rural Minnesota. In case they hadn't, she'd make a stop at the drug store to grab some from their limited selection.

"If she needs anything else, I'll have to find more paper," she said to herself.

Knowing she'd go crazy pacing in the apartment for the next three hours, Brooke made a deal with herself. If she did a five-mile run, she could come home and pretend to read ahead in her accounting textbook while snacking on cookies until Jordan got home. The idea appealed so much, she'd changed into her running gear and was out the door in five minutes.

She was stretching behind the building when she saw Caleb Quentin sneaking out the side door. The teenager, a short kid with shaggy hair, was dressed nicely in slacks instead of jeans, and a simple, white collared golf shirt. "Good morning, Caleb."

He jumped at the greeting. "Oh, hi, Ms. Portman. How's it going?"

"Fine. You're looking good."

Caleb tugged at his collar. "Thanks. I've got an interview at By the Cup. Now that all the summer students are back in school, they need full-time staff."

Brooke sympathized. Finding full-time work in a small town was a job in itself. She'd been fortunate, but she'd learned in the spring she was only one decision from being in Caleb's position, which was why she was going to back to school. "Good luck!"

"Thanks."

Brooke stretched, then started a slow pace toward the lake. She hit Lakeside Drive a block before Castor Marina on the edge of town, jogged past the mostly empty slips, and turned onto Shakespeare Drive, a long and winding street that ran around Star Lake to the Bonfire Bay Campground. It was a scenic route, with cottages lining both sides of the road.

She stopped at a park that was at the halfway mark and pulled out her water bottle. When she heard a car pull into the parking lot behind her, she didn't even have to turn around to know who it was, but she did anyway. She pushed her sweaty bangs off her forehead. "Hi, Aaron."

He rolled down the cruiser's window, and Brooke spotted his hat on the passenger seat. "Aren't you supposed to be out shopping with Jordan?" he asked.

"This afternoon. What are you doing out this way? There can't be any problems here. Yours is the first vehicle I've seen." It wasn't surprising. Most of the cabins had been shuttered for the year when the owners left on Labor Day. Some families would come out a few more times before closing their cottages down for the winter, but Brooke only knew of a handful that were used year-round.

"I was just checking to make sure that Bonfire Bay didn't have any trouble with Labor Day campers."

"Did they?"

"No. One family ended up staying a day longer than they intended due to car trouble, but they got on their way this morning."

"It's always good when Holiday Beach survives yet another summer tourist season."

"It is. The campground did a booming business according to Bernie and Rose. I hear the Dew Drop Inn did too, despite all its changes."

"That was a near thing," Brooke could admit now. In the spring, the hotel had nearly closed its doors before a last-minute change of ownership had breathed new life into the old business. Things were still shifting on a regular basis, but it was all for the better. More importantly, the hotel's occupancy was up, which meant job security for her.

"Then it looks like we're headed into a very good autumn."

He looked so hopeful she couldn't help but agree. "I hope so."

Before the silence between them stretched from awkward to uncomfortable, Aaron's radio squawked. She didn't understand the speaker but apparently, he did. "I've got to go. See you around."

She waved as he pulled away, but once he was out of sight, she shook her head. Flirting without follow-through. Talking about seeing her without asking her out. He left her head spinning, and not in a good way. "That man needs to step up or step off."

CHAPTER 4

AARON SLIPPED into the gymnasium and headed directly to the refreshment table against the back wall. He was dead tired, and if it weren't for the love he had for his son, he'd be home, sprawled on his sofa falling asleep to the dulcet sounds of sportscasters recapping the plays of the week.

Instead, he was at the first Parents of Seniors meeting of the school year, and he had to stay awake for the next two hours. He almost wished for a call to come through to get him out of it, but then he witnessed an interesting sight. His son, who'd been slowly circling the room, made his way over to Brooke and Jordan Portman. He chatted with them for a bit before he and Jordan moved off to talk privately in a different corner of the room.

In seconds, he was standing where his son had been. "That was interesting," he said to Brooke. "Are they, you know..."

"Dating? Not unless they've been doing it online for the last two months. She wasn't seeing Trevor before she left."

"They've only been back in school for two days." Aaron had watched his previously apathetic teenager turn into a student who made himself breakfast and was out the door long before he had to be. Aaron didn't know if the change in attitude was self-directed maturity or orders from the football coach, but he'd take it either way. "Could they have gotten serious so soon?"

"In teenage speak, that's a year, but no, I don't think so." He watched Brooke watch their children, then firmly shake her head and look away. "Are you ready to volunteer for all manner of events tonight? Fundraiser? Trip chaperone?" she asked.

"Snack provider? Chauffeur?" he continued, offering a teasing grin. "Yes, I'm prepared. But Trevor made me promise not to volunteer as a chaperone for any parties or dances. Apparently, having an officer on the scene is a real killjoy."

"You would deprive your son of the chance to watch you perform karaoke in front of his friends?"

Aaron laughed. "He'd never forgive me. How about you? Has Jordan made any requests?"

"No, she's cool with whatever I can do. She knows my options are limited since I'll have night classes."

Roy had mentioned that in passing. Aaron was impressed. It took a lot of nerve and commitment to go back to school so late in the game. "Accounting, right?"

"Bookkeeping. But this fall's course is Accounting 201."

"How are you enjoying it?"

"A lot, surprisingly. It all makes sense to my brain, so I'm not having any trouble picking up the concepts."

The crush around them began to move toward the plastic chairs arranged in front of the auditorium stage.

Aaron ushered Brooke into a row and sat beside her, nodding hello to the other parents.

Principal Kelly introduced the senior student council, representing the hundred or so graduates, and their teacher and parent advisors. The adults in the room wasted no time in getting down to business. The fundraisers for the senior class trip had been decided the previous year, and they were jumping in with both feet.

When they asked for volunteers, Brooke's arm shot into the air. Aaron had been concentrating on his coffee, but he followed her lead and raised his hand as well. "What did we volunteer for?" he asked after they were both recognized.

"Weren't you paying attention?"

"It's been a long week, and I trust you."

"We're in charge of Corn Maze Night."

His eyebrows shot up in surprise. That was a plum assignment, and a lot more fun than decorating the homecoming court parade float. Jackson Farm was a second-generation farm on the outskirts of Holiday Beach. Unlike some of the others in the area that grew organic produce for local sale, Glenna Jackson and her family targeted a different market. They had a massive strawberry field and U-pick business in the early summer, switched to their apple orchard business later in the season, then pivoted again to a pumpkin patch and corn maze in the fall. All their various specialties were family-friendly draws and appealed to the tourists who flocked to Holiday Beach during vacation season.

The profits from the corn maze that they voluntarily gave to the graduating class for one night a year was one of the biggest fundraisers they had. It was so popular that they had to sell tickets in advance of Seniors' Night, and the five hundred available spaces always sold out.

Aaron pulled out his phone "What night is it? I'll make sure I book that night off."

"Night? Singular?" she asked.

"Yes. Why?"

"We're *running the event*," she said with emphasis. "If you want to help, I'll need you on board for more than one night."

He had to work with Brooke Portman on a long-term basis and spend lots of time and evenings with her. That sounded pretty good to him. "My deputies will be happy to cover any time I need off." And if they weren't, he'd encourage them.

Her face brightened at his quick response. "Great! Because I have some ideas on how we can improve on what's been done in past years."

While her enthusiasm was infectious, the parents surrounding her didn't appreciate it. The amount of shushing Brooke endured would have quelled a lesser human, but she persevered until she nailed him down with a time and place for their first committee meeting.

He was still painstakingly typing it into his calendar when he heard his name being called. From the irritation, it didn't sound like it had been the first time. "What was that?" Aaron asked.

"We're a little light on volunteers when it comes to the Homecoming Court Float committee. Can we count on you, Aaron?" Principal Kelly repeated.

Brooke shook her head in small movements. When he looked at her, she opened her eyes widely and mouthed, "Don't do it."

"I'll already be on traffic duty that day, Principal Kelly. I'm sure I'll be able to help again later in the year."

"Good move," Brooke whispered while the principal made his disappointment known.

"Why did I say no to that job?" he whispered back.

"Go ahead. Try to be in charge of four teenaged girls all vying for Homecoming Queen and arguing about who gets the most visible position on the float."

He had his hands full with one teenaged boy. Four girls in the most prestigious, contested social event of their lives was too much for him. "I'm definitely buying the first round of coffee as thanks for that save."

"Let's make it By the Cup tomorrow," she suggested as the meeting broke up. "I'll text you the time."

Aaron raised the phone that was still in his hand. "Can I take a photo for my contact list?" he asked. When she nodded, he quickly snapped a shot of her. He hoped to get a nicer one later, but this one, with her hair back in a simple ponytail, captured her in a casual moment with him that he wanted to remember.

Before he could offer to pose for her, Jordan appeared by her side. "Ready to go, Mom?"

"I'll see you later, Aaron."

"Looking forward to our date."

He smiled when he heard Jordan exclaim as they walked away, "You have a date?"

CHAPTER 5

HER DAUGHTER LOOKED OVERLY serious for a girl with extra marshmallows in her hot chocolate. Brooke didn't know what was going on, but she didn't like it. For the last three days, Jordan had been giving her quizzical looks and making a point of informing her the second her homework was completed.

Now she was poking at her marshmallow foam when she usually scooped it off with a spoon and ate it first. Brooke sighed. Jordan had been under entirely too much stress this year. No kid should have to worry about their parent losing a job. Sure, she wouldn't have been homeless; Jordan knew her father would be happy to have her at any time, and Brooke would have insisted if it came to that. Unfortunately, there was nowhere to hide when you were trying to stretch a dime into a dollar at the grocery store. She'd thought her daughter understood that things were better, that they were back on solid ground, but perhaps she'd been mistaken.

"What's up, Cookie?"

"I'm going to be late after school tomorrow," Jordan said.

"Okay." That wasn't a surprise. Between soccer and volleyball games and practices, working on the school's online paper, and drama club, Jordan rarely came directly home from school.

"Because I'm applying for a job at By the Cup."

Brooke had to have misheard. "Excuse me?"

"I had my first interview with Rachel Best over a video chat while I was visiting Grandma and Grandpa. This is the second. If I get the job, I'll be working two mornings a week from five-thirty to seven thirty, which leaves me half an hour to get to school, and then two evenings, and one weekend day."

"You will be, will you?" They'd had this discussion before. From September till June, Jordan's full-time job was to be a student because grades equalled scholarships. She had regular babysitting gigs all year long and had worked at summer jobs since she was fifteen, including this past summer while she was in New Orleans. In her junior year, she'd also worked one or two weekday evening shifts and weekends at the Fry Guys food truck. They'd never spoken about a regular part-time day job during the week while she was still attending high school, and Brooke thought she'd make her opinions clear.

"My grades are really good, Mom. I have a spare this semester and next semester, so I'll still have lots of time for homework and to study. Even though I'll be applying for scholarships, college will still cost a lot of money. This way I can pay for it without being entirely dependent on student loans."

Brooke bit her tongue. If her seventeen-year-old was

serious—and the arguments she'd provided so far said she was—Brooke only had two options. Shut her down and play the mom card, or treat her like the capable young woman she was trying to raise. It wasn't fair when Jordan made her follow her own rules. "This is something we need to discuss."

"We are discussing it. I waited till I had a second interview to bring it up because otherwise it was a waste of time. This is important to me, Mom."

She was supposed to leave in ten minutes to meet Aaron to have their first in-person volunteer meeting, but this took priority. "You know what your father and I think about you working during the week. That's three shifts beyond what we agreed upon."

"I think I can handle it. They aren't full shifts. They're two hours in the morning and four in the evening. That's twelve hours a week. That's less that the football team practices."

It was a fair point. "What about your other extracurriculars?" Brooke asked.

"I'm going to drop soccer."

"What?" Jordan had played soccer since she was eight and used to climb the goal poles when she was bored.

"It was always secondary to volleyball anyway. Coach Butters thinks we have a chance to make it to state again this year, so I'd miss some soccer practices anyway. I'd rather focus on one thing and do it well."

"What about drama club?"

"Mrs. Bellingham is pregnant and going out on maternity leave in another month, so the winter production is already on hold because no other teachers want to step in. When the spring one is announced, I can reconsider."

Her little girl didn't sound so little when she had all the answers. "What does your dad say?"

"He says that if I get the job, he'll discuss it with you. Don't worry. He already insisted I maintain a minimum A grade in all my classes, or I have to quit."

Brooke was grateful she didn't have to play the heavy on that point. "Then I guess we have to see if you get the job."

Her five-foot-seven daughter almost knocked her off her feet as she sprang at her and pulled her into a hug. "Thanks, Mom. I won't let you down. I'll study extra hard to make up for my work hours. I'll—"

"Get the job first, Cookie. I know you'll do your best. We'll keep a close eye on things and see how you do." Her baby girl wasn't a baby anymore. Didn't that just suck sometimes?

"Why are you all dressed up?"

"I'm meeting Sheriff Gillespie to discuss Corn Maze Night."

Jordan smirked. "Right. You two are working together."

"Why did I hear quotation marks when you said that?" Brooke asked. Now that Jordan was stirring the marshmallow cloud into her cocoa, she was certain the current crisis was over.

"He's handsome, and in uniform, which we both know is your type. Dad likes him."

"How do you know what your dad thinks of him?"

"They're snowmobile buddies. We saw him at the poker derby on St. Patrick's Day." A contemplative look flickered across Jordan's face, but she wiped it away immediately. "He'll be a good person to have on hand at the corn maze in case anybody tries something. And we both know—"

"There's always somebody," they finished together.

Jordan held out Brooke's purse. "Go. Don't be late. Most importantly, remember that the best job is selling popcorn and that you have a daughter who loves you very much."

"Save popcorn duty for Jordan. Got it," Brooke said with a laugh. She scooped her car keys and phone off the breakfast bar and headed out.

She'd planned to arrive at By the Cup early to give herself time to peruse the bakery case. Now she'd barely have time to grab a hot chocolate for herself, which was probably good; Jordan wouldn't appreciate it if she spoke to Rachel Best before her interview. It would be with the best of intentions, but Brooke knew her independent daughter would resent her interference.

For the first time in over a week, she saw Caleb. The eighteen-year-old young man stood behind the counter with a determined look on his face as he entered an order into the tablet in front of him. "It looks like you got the job," Brooke said in greeting when she stepped forward to be served.

"I did!" His pride was evident on his face. "This is my first night alone doing the closing. Rachel's in the office, but I'm in charge."

Brooke took a quick look around the small coffee shop. There were six customers seated at the various tables, plus her and Caleb present. People were spread out across various tables but there were a couple empty ones, and lots of empty chairs and stools. During the morning rush, the small space would be crammed with forty people waiting for their sunrise caffeine fix. With an hour till closing, she didn't see much more business coming through the door. "I'm sure you'll do great."

"Thanks. What can I get you?"

She'd planned to have a hot chocolate since Jordan had put the idea into her head, but then she saw a poster for the seasonal Pumpkin Spice Latte specials, and she couldn't have one of those without a spice muffin.

"I'll call you when it's ready," Caleb said.

When Aaron walked in a minute later carrying a briefcase, she felt woefully underprepared with just her phone on the table. He tucked it under the chair she'd saved for him. "Homecoming parade permits and routes," he said in explanation. "Trevor volunteered to take them into school tomorrow, so I prepared everything this afternoon."

"He volunteered?"

"I swear he was twelve yesterday, bugging me to get him a skateboard. And six the day before, begging me to take his training wheels off. Now he has a driver's license and is willingly going to the principal's office. How did I let that happen?" Aaron demanded, bewildered.

"If it makes you feel any better, before I walked out the door, Jordan hit me with the news that she has an interview for a part-time job. She'd prepared answers for every argument I could think of."

"Ouch, the prepared defense."

"Right? We taught them too well, Aaron. They're young adults now, and we can't make them regress to the kisses and cuddles stage."

"I know. Do you realize what having seniors means?"

"Yeah. It means my high school days weren't five years ago like I keep thinking. They're not even ten." At least it wasn't twenty. She'd had Jordan when she was quite young; she and Denny had married as soon as he received his first posting after boot camp, and Jordan arrived soon after. Still, having a seventeen-year-old meant she was knocking on forty's door.

"Or twenty-five." Aaron fake-coughed into his fist.

That put him at forty-three to her thirty-six. "Ooh, that must have hurt."

"It was this summer, and I've had better weekends."

"At least you look good," Brooke said before she thought about it.

He smiled so big she couldn't backpedal on the compliment. "Thanks."

Caleb called her name before things went awkward. Brooke stuffed an extra dollar in the tip jar as appreciation for his good timing. By the time she got back, Aaron had a file folder on the table.

"I got some maps from Glenna Jackson, including this year's corn maze. I was told to guard it with my life." He slipped a sheet to her, face down.

Brooke flipped it and immediately started laughing at the "TOP SECRET" scrawled across it in orange marker. She stopped when she looked at the maze map. "How long do people have to complete this?" she asked. Suddenly the "We look for people on Mondays and Thursdays" sign they had out last year didn't seem so funny.

"About an hour. Longer if you're doing it in the dark."

"How could you possibly do it in less than two hours?" There were endless loops and intersections. The tower in the middle, which was supposed to let adventurers see where they'd come from and where they were going, would take an hour to reach on its own. Jordan had a personal best time of two hours and seven minutes, and that was a serious improvement over the first time she and her friends had done it while Brooke waited in the rest area.

"The rule of right-hand turns," Aaron said.

Brooke raised her eyebrows in question.

"Really. It's a thing. If you take every right-hand turn, starting at the first turn, you will always find your way out of a corn maze," Aaron insisted. "I don't know how it works, but it does."

"I don't think I trust that. I'd end up shriveled in some corner waiting for the semi-weekly lost-person collection time."

"I'll prove it to you. We'll do the corn maze before Seniors' Night and time ourselves. If I'm wrong and it takes us more than two hours, I'll buy the snacks afterward."

"And if you're right, I'll—"

"Still let me buy the snacks afterward," Aaron insisted. His hazel eyes narrowed slightly, giving him a very determined look.

"Okay."

"How's tomorrow afternoon? We should have a good idea of how long we should expect to give people to complete it if we're going to be running it for the night, even if Glenna will be there."

Her college class hadn't started yet, and Jordan was set for school but wasn't swamped with extracurricular activities. That Saturday afternoon was probably going to be the quietest day on her schedule for the next month. "That sounds good. I'll meet you there."

"No, I can pick you up."

Finally, he was making his move! "I'll be waiting," Brooke said.

CHAPTER 6

SUMMER WAS HANGING on by a thread as Minnesota moved into the second weekend of September. The light layer of dew on Aaron's truck had already burned off, and the sun shone brightly in the clear sky. Yellow leaves dotted the treetops; sometimes an entire branch would be turning gold while the rest stubbornly refused to change. As Aaron enjoyed the view from his front porch, the sounds of a storm grew behind him.

His son burst out of the front door with the keys to the shed in one hand and his car keys in the other. "Bye, Dad."

"Slow your roll, Trev. Where are you going?" He gave his son a lot of freedom, but his teenager liked to see exactly how far he could stretch things. It seemed Trevor's second favorite form of exercise was dancing on his father's last nerve, especially when he leaped before he looked into whatever activity had caught his eye.

Trevor shifted from foot to foot. "Um. Caleb and I are going to cut down some trees."

"Just heading out into the woods with an axe on a

Saturday morning?" Because that sounded like something his son would do.

"No, we're helping Mac cut down some trees on his property." Trevor stopped and stared at him hard. "Remember? Mac Mackenzie asked if I wanted to work with him for a few weekends to clear his property so he can start building his cabin over the winter." The annoyance on his face turned to hurt. "Dad, we had this whole conversation already. You already said it was okay so I told Mac I could work today."

Now Aaron remembered. Trevor had mentioned the local painter looking for some landscaping help. He'd also said something about getting paid in cash and firewood. Considering how many bonfires his son and his friends had in the backyard during the fall, the wood was a big draw. "I forgot. Yes, that's fine."

"Gee, thanks. Again."

He almost said something about the attitude, but he'd started it by assuming Trevor was going to goof off when he was really planning to work. He didn't know if his son realized that clearing a wooded lot meant spending the day getting whacked by branches and slapping at mosquitoes. Then he took note of Trevor's hardy khakis, long-sleeved shirt, and the work boots on his feet and realized the teenager had thought of all of that. "You won't be using a chainsaw, will you?"

"I've used one with you."

"I've shown you how to use one, and you've handled it once. No chainsaw." This time it was an order, not a question or request.

Trevor bristled. "Fine."

Considering how cooperative Trevor had been around the house for the last couple weeks, Aaron decided to cut him a break after bringing down the hammer on the fun of mowing through branches with a rotating blade of death. "You said something about pay and firewood, right?"

"Yeah."

"Do you want to switch vehicles with me and take the truck? I can use your car for my errands, and you don't have to worry about folding seats and trying to fit logs into the back." His son had an ugly but functional ten-year-old SUV that used to belong to his mom. It was safe and held four football players and their gear, but it wasn't meant for hauling firewood.

Aaron's truck, on the other hand, was purchased for outdoor living: camping, fishing, hunting. Unless he was scheduled to work, he never went more than two weekends without taking off into the wild landscape surrounding Holiday Beach.

His offer was met with Trevor's first smile of the morning. "You'd lend me your truck?"

"You're planning to bring home a load of firewood, right? I think it would be more efficient."

"Yes, definitely!"

"Take care of it. Don't park it where it can be hit by falling branches or trees."

"I won't. Thanks, Dad."

Aaron tossed Trevor his keys and caught the ones Trevor threw in return. Before Aaron blinked, Trevor was in the driver's seat and rolling down the driveway. "See you later!"

Aaron waved. He'd have to spend half an hour cleaning Trevor's car so it was in tolerable for his date with Brooke. Knowing Trevor was going to be in the opposite direction to the Jackson Farm let him breathe a little easier. He wasn't ready to let his son know about his date just yet. There might not even be anything to tell him if the afternoon was a bust.

Trevor's car was in worse shape than he anticipated, with more fast food and snack wrappers than was healthy for a teenaged boy. After clearing out the trash, Aaron grabbed paper towels and spray cleaners and wiped down the entire interior. He left the windows open, giving the dashboard a chance to dry and the upholstery an opportunity to get rid of its football funk.

When he arrived at the Remington Apartments, he realized he had no idea which building Brooke lived in. He did notice that the landscaping was in better shape than it had been in previous years, and suspected Lucy Callahan had something to do with it. She seemed to work miracles on the properties under her control. The Dew Drop Inn was practically a new hotel. The apartment buildings where she was the super showed just as much improvement. The cracked planters that used to be on the steps were gone. The iron hand railings had a fresh coat of black paint, and the security window in the door that had been cracked for years was now a flawless piece of sparkling glass.

Matching curtains fluttered behind two second-floor windows in the center building. "Hey, Aaron!" A familiar blonde waved from behind a screen. "I'll be right down."

He got out of the car and had the passenger door open by the time Brooke hit the front step. She was in a short-sleeved, blue plaid shirt and jeans, and she had a light navy jacket in her hand. She was also carrying a backpack that was stuffed to overflowing.

"How much gear are you bringing?" he asked. "We aren't going to be exploring the old Holiday copper mine."

"With my sense of direction, we could end up there."

"Brooke, we'll be in a maze. There are literally walls to ensure we can't escape."

She shrugged. "Don't say I didn't warn you."

The Jackson farm was about fifteen miles south of town, halfway between Bixby and Holiday Beach. They weren't near Star Lake, but the property did have two creeks running it that fed their orchards and fields. The car bumped over ruts that had dried in the mud and stopped in the parking area off the long driveway. On one side was the maze, where seven foot stalks of corn ran for dozens of yards in either direction from the gap under the archway marked "Entrance". At the far end of the parking area was the ticket booth and the snack stand, which offered potato chips and popcorn and drinks and hot dogs. Beside them were picnic tables and firepits for the evening maze-goers.

The maze was open, but there were only a dozen cars this early in the day. Brooke gave the sky a serious look, then tied the jacket around her waist. "I'm ready to spend the rest of my days lost and wandering until my death." She sniffed dramatically. "Lead me to my doom, Aaron Gillespie. I'll be fine."

"Way to go with the confidence, Brooke." Her dark humor was a new side he'd never seen, but it was funny. "I need to get our passes before we get to the doom."

"Good planning. We don't want to die horribly before handing over our cash."

He was still laughing when he paid for two tickets. Glenna Jackson stood behind the counter. The tall Black woman was agog at his approach. "Did you actually get Brooke to agree to go into the maze?" she asked as she took his money.

"She says she comes here every year with Jordan," Aaron said.

"Comes here, yes. Enters the maze, never. She sits in the snack area and waits for the kids to finish."

"Not this year," Aaron said.

"If you lose her in there, she will haunt you forever."

"I'll keep her close," he promised.

He returned with their wristbands. "Do you want to get some popcorn to take with us?" he asked as he fastened hers around her outstretched hand.

"So a murder of crows can attack and chase us deeper into the cornfields? No thanks."

His laughter exploded. "What is up with you? Why did you say you'd come if you hate corn mazes so much?"

"Because you asked. Besides, I don't hate them. I just have a highly honed Halloween spooky meter and an honorary master's degree in horror movies. Corn mazes are a solid eight on the meter. Eight-and-a-half if you do them after dark. Nine if there are children in them after sunset. Those high-pitched giggles and screams in the dark? The rustling corn stalks when the wind blows? Creepy."

"Why on earth would you volunteer for this fundraiser?"

"Free popcorn, obviously. Besides, I don't have to actually go into the maze that night. I can supervise and sell tickets from out here."

"Well, I already paid for the tickets. I guess you'll have to trust me."

Brooke paused as they stood under the entrance sign and pulled out her phone.

"You aren't setting a GPS position, are you?" he

asked. There was prepared, and there was paranoia, and he didn't know which way Brooke was leaning.

"That's a good idea, but no. I'm starting the clock. You said this right-hand plan of yours means it'll take less than two hours for us to finish, right?"

"Right."

She pressed a couple buttons. "I just started the timer. Let's go." She reached back and grabbed his hand, then pulled him over the threshold.

Her fingers relaxed a couple steps in, but Aaron kept a hold of her. She'd started it, but he wasn't above taking advantage. The early afternoon sun was warm, and the corn blocked the breeze they'd felt in the parking lot. It was a beautiful day for a walk with a beautiful woman.

Whoever designed the maze had a sense of humor he wasn't prepared for. About ten yards in, they came to a crossroads, with the three directions labeled as "Oz," "Narnia," and "Wonderland".

"What's your choice?" he asked.

She pointed to Wonderland. "You said turn right. That's the plan, right?"

"It works, but you have to turn right every single time. No exceptions."

"What if you find yourself in a dead end?"

"You turn right. Facing corn? Turn right you're moving again. Then right at the next option," he said.

Brooke screwed up her face. "That sounds fishy."

"You promised you'd try it."

"I did. So, off to Wonderland," she said.

There was lots of laughter as they got started. At one point, they stood aside as a mob of tweens wearing matching T-shirts raced past them, then split into two groups at the next junction.

"How's Jordan doing in school?" he asked.

"Mostly okay." She made a face. "She has Mr. Tambo for English next semester."

He knew Matt Tambo. The teacher was a middle-aged, middle-class man who Aaron didn't interact with except for at speed traps on the highway. "Is there a problem with him?"

"A couple years ago, he and Glenna Jackson got into it at a school board meeting. He insisted that *Huckleberry Finn* was a classic and should be mandatory. Glenna said that every year he called on the Black students in his classroom to read the most profane excerpts aloud. His reasoning was that since they were the ones speaking the n-word, it made it okay. Glenna said it was a racist excuse. She convinced the board, and they dropped the book from the curriculum."

"I didn't know that."

"Eli, her youngest, graduated this past June. A week ago, Mr. Tambo proposed changes for next semester's book list. He's pushing for *To Kill a Mockingbird*. Do you remember it?"

He shrugged. "Vaguely."

"I reread it as soon as I heard about it. There are only *slightly* fewer instances of racial slurs. Now Denny and I are speaking at the next school board meeting. Glenna's already done most of the hard work, but it never ends. There are so few Black students in the school that teachers like Mr. Tambo tend to slip through. My daughter should not have to fight in this day and age."

"How ugly is this going to get? Can I do anything?"

"Do you want to sit in at the board meeting? Your presence may help keep tempers in check."

"Unless I get called out, I'll be there."

"But aside from that, Jordan loves being a senior. She especially loves working on the online school paper this year because, apparently, seniors get assigned all the best stories. No word on any exposés so far, but I won't be surprised if she uncovers one."

"I wish Trevor would get more involved in extracurriculars, and not just for his college applications. Aside from football, his circle of friends is pretty small."

"Is he grounded again? Is that why you have his car?"

"Not this time. He's doing some outdoor work today and needed the truck to haul firewood, so we traded."

"Firewood," Brooke said with a sigh. "That's one thing I really don't like about our apartment—no fireplace."

"We have a firepit," Aaron said, an idea forming instantly. "We should have you and Jordan over sometime. Maybe some kind of thank you for the other volunteers." It would kill two birds with one stone: get Brooke to his place and get Jordan and Trevor used to seeing them together.

"That sounds like fun."

Now all he had to do was convince his son. "Great."

"Great," Brooke echoed, her voice flat and unimpressed.

That's when he noticed they'd walked into a dead end. "Not a problem. Don't panic. Remember the plan."

"We've only been walking for five minutes."

"Then we won't have lost much time."

"If this doesn't work and we have to resort to cannibalism to survive, people are going to start calling you Lefty Leg Gillespie," Brooke warned.

"So noted." She was teasing when she said it, but there was a tightness around her eyes that hadn't been there a minute ago. Aaron reached for her hand again. "Come on. We'll be at the center lookout before you know it, and we'll be able to gloat over how quickly we got there."

She gave him a determined nod. "Okay. We can do this. Next stop, the lookout."

The Jacksons had had fun when they'd set up the maze. Every five minutes or so, they came across a small sign painted with a joke-telling jack-o-lantern. The first one made the corners of Brooke's mouth twitch. The second got a chuckle. The puns got progressively worse the further they went. Brooke insisted on taking a picture of every one of them. "I won't post them on social media till we're a lot closer to Halloween, so I don't spoil the fun, but they're too adorable not to share," she told him.

Thirty minutes later—they'd hit two more dead ends —they climbed the two-storey staircase to stand on the large wooden platform that overlooked the property. The corn was so tall it blocked sight of most of the people, but every now and then a flash of color appeared in a gap. The concession stand was doing good business, and the picnic tables were more crowded than they'd been when he and Brooke had begun. He pointed at another group emerging from the maze and raising their arms in victory.

"Wow, this is some view," Brooke said.

She was facing the other direction, facing the apple orchard that had been full of red a month ago was down to sporadic dots among the thinning, dark green leaves. Beyond that, rows of ankle-high green and brown strawberry plants poked up between rows of straw. Now that the trees were starting to shed their foliage, they caught glimpses of the creek that ran through the back of the property.

The sun caught her brown eyes, and, for a moment, they looked like glittering pieces of amber. The wind blew a few whisps of hair across her cheek, and she absently brushed them away.

"Gorgeous." He wasn't talking about the scenery.

She turned, then grabbed his arm. "Hey, look!" She pointed at the path they had to take to start the second half of the journey. Her finger wound and twisted in the air. "The next right we have to take—" Brooke cut herself off, then checked that they were still alone. "We're going to hit a dead end in three more turns, but then there's a good long stretch."

"Shall we get to it?"

"Absolutely. We still have eighty-two minutes before you have to buy my popcorn."

Her cutthroat competitive streak bubbled to the surface when the T-shirt gang from the beginning of the maze caught them again at the base of the tower. "Say, Aaron, doesn't the secret map you got say the shortcut is that way?" she said, pointing left.

The herd immediately raced past them and entered the left-hand branch of the path.

"Come on, let's beat those little turkeys," she said as she darted right.

He had to run to catch up.

They burst through the exit twenty-five-and-a-half minutes later, a single turn ahead of the mob of kids who were hot on their trail. Sweat slicked his hair to his forehead as he pulled Brooke out of the way of the thundering stampede.

"We did it!" He was stunned when Brooke wrapped her arms round him in a hug. Not too stunned to hug her back, but he was surprised by the emotion she was willing to show him. She seemed to realize what she'd done, though, and quickly let him go and stepped away.

Brooke checked her phone and cleared her throat. "Fifty-two minutes. That beats Jordan's best time by over an hour. She's going to flip when I tell her that I stomped her record to dust on my first attempt."

"Are you going to tell her about the right-hand turn trick?"

"No way! That's our secret. We can't have her busting our new record in the same year."

"That sounds fair."

The air was cooler and breezier now that they were back in the open. The sun had begun its decline even though it was only midafternoon. The tops of the trees were starting to throw shadows. By the time he was through the concession line and had returned with their coffees and popcorn, Brooke had staked out a small table upwind from one of the still-dark firepits.

"This was fun, but we're also here to work. Let's chat about the fundraiser," she proposed.

As they discussed the number of people who came through on an average night and the various positions that needed to be filled, the scope of the project hit home. They needed people directing cars in the parking lot, ticket sellers, people counting how many went in and came out of the maze, concession workers, and a clean-up detail. "This is going to take half of the senior class."

"Pretty close," Brooke agreed.

Glenna joined them near the end and offered a couple refinements to their plan. They agreed to contact her in another week with the finalized details. Glenna gave Brooke a hug and offered her hand to Aaron.

The drive home was much too short. Aaron pulled in

front of Brooke's apartment. "I had a lot of fun this afternoon."

"I did too. I can't believe you got me into the corn maze."

"I'm a trustworthy guy."

"You must be."

"I'd love to do it again sometime." He let the silence stretch, giving her a chance to respond.

"Me too. But there are other considerations."

There were lots of them. His son. Her daughter. His job. Her night classes. "There are, but I think exploring what we have—what we could have—is worth the risk. And the effort. How about you?"

She nodded. "It's been just me and Jordan for a while now, but I think we're both ready for me to be open to the idea of someone new in my life."

"I think we should investigate this idea," he agreed. They weren't making a lifelong commitment at this point. They didn't even know if what they had would go anywhere. All they were sure of was that they got along and liked each other, but it was a long way to go from a single date to dating.

"So, let's investigate," Brooke said.

CHAPTER 7

"WHY ARE my feet killing me? I've been on them for longer stretches of time at soccer tournaments." Jordan lifted her feet to the arm of the sofa and wriggled her bare toes. After spending four hours on her feet running coffee to customers, she came home and announced her first paycheck was going towards better shoes. Brooke sympathized. Service jobs were hard on several levels, and physical was one of the biggest.

"Use some peppermint foot lotion before you go to bed." But she still wanted to spend time with her daughter. Since Jordan's phone was charging on the kitchen island and her feet were too sore for her to run away, she had a captive audience. "How's the student paper?"

"Fine. Pretty slow right now since it's the beginning of the year."

"No big stories in the works?"

"I'm working on an opinion piece for next week's edition about the school board's sexist student policies, but I'm not ready to talk about it yet."

Strike one. "Let me know when it's ready. I'd love to

read it." *And find out why I'm going to be called down to the principal's office,* Brooke added in her head. She knew Jordan would have the facts to support her comments, but that topic sounded like it was going to ruffle a few feathers. "How's the social situation? Any new students? Any old students come back with a new look?"

"Anybody date-worthy?" Jordan translated. She rolled her eyes. "No, Mom. Just the same people I've been going to school with for the last four years. If I haven't dated them by now, I'm not going to. Plus, I'm a senior. I can't go out with a sophomore."

Strike two. "Have you started filling out any college applications?"

"Mom! It's September!"

Strike three. Just because she had time with her teenager didn't mean she was going to receive a flood of information from her. Which meant Jordan was perfectly normal. "I want you to know, it will be discussed at length at Thanksgiving with your father. You might want to have an idea about where you want to go, or at least apply."

"I will."

Brooke retired to their tiny bathroom. She turned on the hot water tap and let it run, adding a sprinkle of citrus-scented Epsom salts and a splash of baby oil. The tub was small, but she'd have half an hour of uninterrupted soaking time.

She texted back and forth with Aaron till they agreed on a day and time for dinner: Friday, seven o'clock, at the Atlas Restaurant. After she'd texted him good night, she set her phone on the vanity and submerged her head under the hot water.

She had a date.

Brooke quickly surfaced, sputtering.

She needed clothes.

———

Three days later, she took one last look in the mirror. The toes of her black dress boots stuck out from her jean cuffs. They accentuated the leather accents from the black and silver belt Lucy had lent her. Her blouse was a fitted, long-sleeve shirt of a deep red with a hint of orange, like the leaves of a maple at this time of year. Her blonde hair was back in a ponytail, with small, jeweled hairpins keeping it sleek and adding a little sparkle. "Is it too much? Or not enough?"

"You look great," Lucy Callahan said from her corner of the sofa.

"Your hair is stunning. Aaron won't know what hit him," Mina Blackburn added.

Her two friends helped settle her nerves. That was why she'd invited them over.

It was Friday night. Jordan was at By the Cup, working till closing. Brooke had the apartment for another hour before Aaron would pick her up, and she'd called in some moral support. "I don't know why I'm so nervous," she said. "It's a first date."

"That he's been flirting toward since April," Lucy said. Evidently, she planned to spend a quiet night at home alone. She was wearing a hoodie with frayed cuffs and yoga pants. Her blue eyes didn't pop as much as they usually did since she wasn't wearing any makeup.

Lucy would know about flirting; Brooke had called her months ago asking if the signals Aaron had giving were of the interested variety. Lucy assured her they were. For weeks, Brooke had become more and more frustrated as Aaron refused to take the next step. Now her nerves were telling her she'd been too hasty.

"Flirting? Why didn't I hear about the flirting?" Mina demanded. She was dressed like she did have a date later, but Mina always looked good. Her hair was a glossy black that looked like she'd just come out of a salon, even if it was in a simple French braid like she was currently wearing. She had on a purple sweater that matched her violet eyes, and a lipstick that was a few shades darker than both.

"If you haven't heard anything, you're the only person in town," Brooke countered. "Lucy and Roy have been teasing me mercilessly."

"Where have I been?"

"Working," Brooke told her. While Lucy had become a good friend in the months since she'd come to town, Mina had been her best friend for years. The Starlight Gallery had begun as a seasonal artisans' shop, catering to the summer tourist crowd. With a lot of work, Mina had moved it to a permanent, year-round location and added an internet shop. Then she'd expanded with an attached stained glass studio.

Lucy picked up her wineglass for a sip of chardonnay. "We really have been annoying, but we tease with love."

"I can understand being out of the general loop. I've been working nonstop putting the show together, but I don't understand why didn't *you* tell me? This rates at least a text," Mina said.

"You've been there the few times I dipped my toes back into the dating pool. I wanted to make sure this time I was ready to dive in."

"Are you ready?"

"Splash" was her simple answer.

"Well, you'd better put on your water wings and take a deep breath, my friend, because the sheriff has arrived." Lucy unfolded her legs from beneath her. "Let's go back to my apartment, Mina. There's a new episode of *Dress for Success* tonight, and Pieros is a magician when it comes to his hairstyles during the makeover portion."

"Do you want to follow it with *The Creative Baker*?"

"It's too soon for me to watch baking shows. I'm still not over the creations from the Junior Shamrock Baking Championship," Lucy said as she grabbed her keys.

Brooke snickered. Lucy had a green tongue for days after being a judge at that preteen cooking contest.

"You laugh, but every good relationship has at least one memorable date." Lucy made it sound like a threat. "Go, keep that little tidbit in the back of your mind while you're enjoying your night out with Aaron."

Brooke was too busy slipping into her heels and giving her hair one last glance to respond. Fortunately, Mina did it for her. "You're mean, Lucy."

She looked up in time to see Lucy grin at her. "But I'm mean with love."

CHAPTER 8

HOLIDAY BEACH WASN'T big enough to support an exclusive, expensive restaurant. Aaron had done the best he could, reserving a table in the Atlas's dining room rather than the main restaurant. It was a little quieter, carpeted instead of tiled, and each table had the illusion of privacy. The Atlas's owners, Tripp Turner and his wife Habibah Gamal, had given him one of the booths. A small bowl of yellow, orange and white mums sat in the center of the table. A lit tealight augmented the dim light from the sconces on the wall.

Tripp waited on them personally. "Good evening, Aaron and Brooke. You're both looking well tonight. Would you like to hear our specials before I take your drink orders?" The former soldier's eyes twinkled as he addressed them with such formality.

"By all means, please go ahead," Brooke responded in kind while Aaron tried not to snicker into his water glass.

Tripp reeled off two kinds of soup—corn chowder and chicken with wild rice—then two entrees—butternut squash ravioli and short ribs—and offered a choice of apple crumble or chocolate cake for dessert.

"I'm going to need some time," Brooke told him.

Tripp grinned and nodded, and slipped away silently, with only the slightest limp giving away his old injury.

"Thanks for that," Aaron said. "I need a moment too. I'm having the chicken with rice and the ravioli, but having to pick only one of Habibah's desserts is a terrible choice to make." He could handle a grill and a can opener, but baking pans were beyond him. Trevor had a light touch when it came to muffin-making, but he and his son were two of the reasons why Holiday Beach's two bakeries stayed in business.

Brooke stared at him like he'd grown a second head. "You can't be serious."

"About what?"

"If it's September, you always go for the apple crumble. How do you not know this?"

An older couple, the man inexplicably wearing bowling shoes, paused as they walked by their table. "She's right, you know. Always choose the apple crumble at this time of year."

Aaron lay his menu on the corner of the table. "I guess I don't have a problem deciding after all."

That was how they started the meal. Over soup, he discovered that while Brooke had no love of winter sports, she and Jordan regularly hiked around Star Lake on the various public trails. She was open to the idea of fishing, on the understanding that someone else cleaned whatever was caught and presented her with the fillets for frying.

"You know, that is part of the process," he tried to argue. It wasn't his favorite part either, but he'd taught Trevor how to do it a couple years ago

"I don't butcher my own cows or pluck my own chickens either," she countered.

So many people deferred to him because of his badge or challenged him despite it. It was nice to have someone treat him as a regular man, a potential date, and fellow parent of teenagers. As he and Brooke danced from topic to topic, the lingering tension about his job slowly eased.

Until an unwelcome and uninvited figure appeared at the end of their table as Tripp cleared the remains of an amazing dinner away. "Can I help you, Neil?" he asked, his tone telling the interloper that the proper response was "Not at all, I was just leaving."

"You could do your job, Sheriff."

Brooke bristled at the other man's tone. "Neil Dempsey, we said hello to you in the lobby when we were waiting to be seated. You sat over there and had salad, meat loaf, and chocolate cake for dessert. You're only standing here complaining now because you've finished your meal. If it was an emergency, you've had over an hour to come talk to Aaron. You didn't," Brooke said in a voice that had both men a little intimidated.

"Is it an emergency, Neil?"

The cottage owner looked from him, to Brooke, then back. "Not exactly."

"Would you like to come into the office tomorrow and make an official report?"

"I want you to find the thief that's been hitting the cottages along Shakespeare Drive."

Brooke stilled beside him. "Really? There's a thief?" she asked quietly.

He patted her hand while keeping his eyes on Neil. "Your case of six missing pieces of firewood at the

Dickens Estate has been noted. However, since both your wife and your kids say that they shifted the logs back and forth when you winterized your cabin on Labor Day, no one was certain as to whether or not they left a small pile by the firepit. Is something else missing?" He couldn't simply write the man off; cottages were often a target for break-ins since they were unoccupied for long stretches. But small amounts of firewood were not a good source of income for criminal masterminds.

"The tarp that the Austin Cottage uses to cover their glider swing is missing. Then there were four old tires by the road at Shelley's Shack, and there are two now. Somebody is robbing those cottages blind."

"I am not investigating missing trash, Neil. Especially when it was left out for pick up. Was the glider swing still there?"

"Well, yes—"

"Then I suggest you have a good night and file another formal report in the morning. I'd hate for you to get so agitated that you get indigestion after Habibah's meatloaf." Aaron raised his hand to hold off another flood of complaints. "I'll go take a look around, but if nothing has been taken, I can't do anything."

When Brooke hesitated after Tripp asked if they wanted dessert, Aaron knew he had to say something. "Don't even think about skipping the apple crumble. Neil's situation is not an emergency. Sadly, stuff like this happens a lot."

"People being jerks to you in the middle of a restaurant?"

"People informing me about whatever, whenever," he clarified. "Robberies in the restaurant parking lot, noise complaints at the grocery store, parking tickets at the football game. Even when I'm out of uniform, the badge really never goes away." It was one of the biggest downsides of the job. As much as he wanted to impress Brooke, he wasn't going to lie about things that would affect whoever he was seeing. Although he did wish he'd managed to get through his first date without having it thrown in her face.

"That doesn't sound like much fun."

"Nine out of ten times, it's not. Sometimes it's a thank you, or a real emergency when the interruption means I'm in time to stop something really bad from happening. Those make up for the rest. Except when I'm on a date with a beautiful woman. It would have to be supremely important to top that."

A slow smile pulled at the corners of Brooke's mouth, then spread into a full grin. "On the other hand, this does provide you with a unique dating opportunity that most men can never offer," she said.

Like any experienced law enforcement professional, Aaron recognized when he was entering a dangerous but unknown situation, and Brooke definitely qualified. "What's that?"

"You can deputize me and bring me as backup when you go to investigate those burglaries on Shakespeare Drive." Her eyes were alight at the thought.

Aaron hadn't been so scared in years. "Not a chance."

———

"You are not my deputy, and this is not a ride-along. We are simply going for a nice, unofficial evening drive to admire the autumn foliage along the lakeshore," Aaron said for the third time. At least this time he got all the words out before his passenger started to snicker.

"Foliage," Brooke echoed.

"I'm serious. I am not on duty. You wouldn't be anywhere near here if Neil was anybody else. I'd never endanger you by bringing you to a potential crime scene."

"There is no crime. Just foliage," Brooke said, giggling. Then she sat straight in her seat. "There." She pointed to the wooden sign at the end of a driveway.

Like the other cottages along Shakespeare Drive, Austen Cottage was labelled with a sign naming the cottage, not the family who lived there. It was a strange quirk, but the town's summer guests loved it and had continued the tradition as new properties were built around the lake.

Austen Cottage was a cottage in name only. The two-storey house on stilts had been around for sixty years. It was well maintained but not upgraded, which meant it had passed through old and become vintage with an unmistakable sixties vibe. The glider swing, a massive steel and wood double swing that sat six comfortably, had a prime view of Star Lake. The cottage owners usually threw a large orange tarp over the structure to protect the wooden seat slats over the winter. But Neil was right; it was bare and open to the elements.

"Shall we take a quick look for the tarp?" Brooke asked. "It would be hard to miss."

The sun was low on the horizon, and soon it would go from evening to dusk to dark. They didn't see the covering caught in any underbrush as they walked along the perimeter of the property. It also wasn't wrapped around any of the house's stilts or used to cover any of the seasonal toys the family stored there.

"I hate to think it blew into the lake," Aaron said. They tried to keep people from dumping trash in the lake, but accidents happened.

"I didn't see any rope," Brooke said.

Aaron returned to the swing. She was right. There was no rope tied around the swing frame. No bungee cords hung awkwardly from the seat or lay half anchored under the base. "Maybe they forgot this year," he said. Neither of them believed it.

"Tires next?" Brooke asked.

Shelley's Shack was named after the author of *Frankenstein*, and the building was as monstrous as the creature it was named after. He hadn't seen any activity on the property over the last summer. What was supposed to be the lawn was a field of overgrown and dying weeds. The roof sagged heavily in the middle, and missing boards on the exterior offered glimpses of tattered tar paper and discolored insulation. Heavy, dark blankets hung in front of all the windows, blocking any view of the interior. Aaron doubted the building could pass an inspection, but that wasn't why he was here.

Four rings of dead grass lined the ditch where the driveway met the road. "I don't think the Pineys were the ones who set out the tires, but it looks like somebody took the other two. At least they're not in a dump somewhere," he said.

"If they're on the side of the road somewhere, that's not stealing, is it?" Brooke asked.

"No. They're actually saving Shelley's Shack from a littering charge."

"What else was there? Missing firewood?"

"Neil can't even confirm anything was missing. A ten-minute walk through the woods will provide more than enough fallen branches for a bonfire." They weren't in the wilderness, although Star Lake was on the edge of a heavily treed and hilly area that spread north.

"I can see him being too cheap to buy firewood."

They stopped by a couple other properties Aaron knew to be empty. All the windows were closed; the doors were locked with no sign of tampering. "This was a wild-goose chase. I'm sorry it wasted so much of our evening," he said to Brooke. He'd waited months for this chance with her. This was not the impression he'd hoped to make.

"I thought we were having a good time. I mean, I'd rather not spend every date rushing through dessert so we can investigate potential crime"—she cut herself off—"I mean, criminally beautiful foliage, but it makes a good first date story. Assuming there's going to be a second, more traditional date that follows this one."

Aaron released a sigh that let his shoulders drop a full inch. Her attitude was a great start. It was a lot different to live with his job day in and day out, but if it started this well, they had a chance to move forward. "I *was* planning on a second date."

"Good. Ask me when we get home."

The streetlights were on when he pulled to a stop in front of her apartment block. Aaron glanced at her building. Although all the security lights were on, there were still more shaded areas than he was comfortable with. "Is that Caleb Quintin? Does he live here?"

"Yeah. He graduated in June, but he was in a few of Jordan's classes last year. He's working at By the Cup these days. Jordan has had a couple shifts with him."

"I don't have a problem with him. His parents..." He stopped to think. "Well, his parents haven't been causing problems lately, actually. I haven't had a noise complaint in a couple months, and Roy hasn't called either." Roy did a good job of handling troublemakers at the Escape Room, but every now and again, some people tried to push their luck.

"Before you head up to your apartment, let's talk about us. When can I see you again?" he asked, now that his mind was at ease.

"Not Monday. I have—"

"Accounting class," they said together.

"How about Tuesday?" he asked.

"I have a late work shift and then homework. I'm in an online study group to review the previous day's lesson. Wednesday?"

"I have a homecoming meeting on Wednesday to discuss the parade route. How about Thursday?" he countered.

"There's a volunteer meeting on Thursday night to organize the details of Corn Maze Night," she continued.

"Right. I forgot."

"Friday?" she asked.

He hesitated. Technically he was off, but he'd already said he was in for the semi-regular poker game the guys held. Roy Wagner, Tripp Turner, and some of the others. "Technically, it's poker night. Do you want to come along?"

"That's sweet, but no thank you, twice. First, I have no poker face whatsoever, so I might as well give you my money now. Second, if you have plans with the guys, you shouldn't cancel them for me. There's a whole calendar left that we can look at."

"Saturday?" Aaron suggested.

"I'm free on Saturday."

"Me too."

"Great." He leaned across the console dividing their seats. When she smiled at him, he leaned closer and gave her a quick kiss. "Really great."

"Really, really great," she agreed.

CHAPTER 9

BROOKE'S SMILE when she saw him on Friday night was genuine, but underneath that, she looked exhausted. Aaron quickly adjusted his plans, glad they hadn't scheduled something special in advance. "Instead of a movie in Bixby, would you like to take another drive through the foliage?" he asked. A slow cruise around Star Lake would be plenty romantic on a clear, moonlit night like they had before them.

"If you don't mind a shorter evening, that would be great. It's been a week," she admitted.

"Want to tell me about it?" He'd already bought her a Pumpkin Spice Latte, anticipating that they'd be in his truck for at least half an hour no matter what they decided to do.

She carefully peeled back the lid. "Jordan's first op-ed came out in the student paper this week. On the question whether or not there was gender bias in the school's dress code, she came down firmly on the side of yes, there was, and the girls shouldn't have to suffer under some archaic regulations. She also had some good supportive quotes from other students, including your son."

Aaron had no idea Trevor had participated in a story, even as an interviewee. His son kept surprising him lately. "I'd like to read it."

"I'll send you the link."

He grimaced when the radio squawked. "Sorry, I have to leave it on. I'm on call tonight."

Brooke gave him another smile. "Remember, I'm always available to be deputized."

"Not a chance."

The sun was long down, but it was unseasonably mild, so they had the windows down. With the still air and the clear sky, it was a beautiful night to be out with a beautiful woman.

The drive was as relaxing as he'd hoped. Brooke's head was on a swivel as she admired the stars and the reflection of the moon on the lake and the silhouettes of the bare birch branches against the darker trees. "I love fall," she said. "The crispness in the air and the crunch of leaves under your feet. Then it ends by rolling into Thanksgiving and Christmas, which is like the best season finale ever."

"Winter ends with an explosion of greenery and the end of shoveling. Spring ends with fireworks."

"They're all the best season finales, but this is the one we have right now. Let me enjoy a lovely fall drive with my boyfriend, would you?"

He liked the sound of being her boyfriend. "Sorry, ma'am."

"Mm, the smell of woodsmoke. I love the smell of a fire."

The night sky was bright enough to find the trail of

smoke from the campfire. Aaron judged the distance and the direction and realized it was coming from Shelley's Shack. Which wouldn't be a problem except that the Piney family had specifically told him earlier in the summer they weren't expecting to be back in Holiday Beach for the rest of the year.

"If I ordered you to stay in the car, would you stay in the car?" he asked.

"I'm not your deputy, so I don't have to follow your orders."

Aaron expected that. "What if I asked nicely?"

"I'd consider it if you told me why."

"That bonfire is at Shelley's Shack, and nobody's supposed to be there. I suspect that if I show up, we're going to find a party with a bunch of people who shouldn't be there. Trevor had better pray he's not one of them."

"Are you going to call for backup?"

"I'll let the station know where I am."

"Then I'll stay in the car." His face must have shown his surprise. "Hey, I can be reasonable," Brooke insisted.

The partygoers had enough brains not to park in the driveway, but they weren't smart enough to realize he could record the licences plates parked on the street. He left Brooke in the car, and carefully stalked around the dilapidated cabin to the firepit in the back. Half a dozen people were around the roaring bonfire, some on lawn furniture that Aaron knew didn't belong there. Beer bottles clinked in the dark, and somebody yelled, "Yeah, throw that in the fire." Then the silhouette of a picnic table bench appeared in the air.

"No. Set it down," he said firmly. He turned on the flashlight and shone it in each of their faces. It wasn't to get a better look; Aaron already recognized almost everyone there. Students and recent graduates from Holiday Beach's high school whom he already had a passing, professional history with.

"We've got cops!"

They scattered like rats when the lights came on. Three raced for the far side of the cabin. One stumbled farther into the dark and the brush. From the noise he made, Aaron would have lots of time to go back and find him. The guy holding the bench dropped it, just missing the fire. As he watched the other man eye him, Aaron shifted his feet and braced himself. This guy was going to charge him and try to knock him over on his way by.

Aaron, however, wasn't six beers to the wind. Unfortunately, he was also six inches shorter and a hundred pounds lighter, so skill and sobriety were less helpful than momentum.

Aaron's boots left the ground. He bounced off the cabin wall and landed on them flatfooted. He needed to take a breath before he started his pursuit.

He could have taken two. Because the guy he was chasing ran out of gas halfway down the driveway and was puking into the bushes. Aaron waited for both their sakes before cuffing him and sitting him on the side of the road.

Of the entire mess, the best thing was seeing Brooke in his truck, knocking on the window to get his attention. "Can I come out now?" she yelled.

Blue lights flashed in the distance, coming closer. "Give me one more minute, hun."

After ensuring the bench guy wasn't going to be sick in the cruiser, he handed him over to the deputy on duty. Then the guy who'd run into the woods stumbled onto the road, now bleeding from scrapes on his face and arms. He joined his buddy.

He promised to go to the station shortly to make a statement. First, he wanted to check out the cabin and see what damage the group had caused. After he cleared the building, he let Brooke join him.

"What a mess," she groaned.

The partiers had done a real number on the property. Another bench had already been fed to the fire. Charred legs stuck out of the other side of the pit. A destroyed bright red Adirondack chair lay in pieces beside it, also ready for burning.

"I don't remember that being back here," Brooke said.

"It wasn't. If I'm not mistaken, the benches are from Hemingway's Hideaway, and the chair is from Austen Cottage."

"Neil's going to flip."

"Especially when he learns his son was part of it."

Aaron caught her flinch even in the growing dark. "Have fun with that conversation," she muttered.

"Can you hold some boards when I nail this board shut?" he asked. He felt bad for the Pineys. The footprint on the back door and the splintered jamb meant they were in for some serious expenses.

"Is there any damage inside?" Brooke asked.

"It's a mess, but I can't tell if anything is missing."

She pulled out her phone and activated the flashlight to see inside. Table chairs lay on their sides. The fireplace mantle was empty, but the floor was littered with candles and broken hurricane lamps. A shelf in the bathroom that looked like it had been torn from the wall above the toilet lay in the bottom of the shower. "Yep, it's a wreck in there."

Aaron asked her to hold her phone light while he hammered the slats from the broken Adirondack chair to hold the door in place. "That'll hold it till morning."

As they walked back to his truck, she slipped her arm around his. "You take me to the nicest crime scenes."

Aaron groaned. "That's it. No more foliage for you."

"No, don't take away the foliage!"

They chatted all the way back to town, and he parked in the visitor spot behind her building. "Have you noticed how many of our dates end up with me having to cut them short to go to the station?"

"That's the job, right?"

It was, but he hadn't resented it like this for a while. "I promise it'll slow down in November."

She reached across the seat and took his hand. "Aaron, we're both adults with busy lives. Your job is more demanding than most, but I knew that going in. When—because I'm sure it will be a when and not an if—it gets to be too much, I promise to talk to you about it. Until then, don't worry. But I do appreciate the consideration."

His previous exhaustion returned, and he had hours of paperwork and calls to make. "Before I go, can you give me a goodnight kiss to remember our criminally good second date?" he requested.

She did.

CHAPTER 10

BROOKE WIPED her hand on the dish towel hanging from the oven door. Her apartment smelled of tomatoes, onion, garlic, and oregano. A jug of water with lime slices sat chilling in the fridge. The table was set with china and silverware, and a basket of rolls. All that was missing was her guest.

When Aaron texted to ask her out to coffee that night, she instead invited him for dinner. It seemed perfectly reasonable at the time. Jordan teased her, saying that since she was working an evening shift, they'd have the small apartment to themselves.

Then Brooke realized it was the first time they'd be alone when they weren't in a vehicle.

She raised her hands to her mouth and huffed into them. Fresh mouthwash wouldn't hurt. As she rinsed and spit, she realized spaghetti sauce with garlic wasn't the most romantic meal.

It was too late now.

She saw Aaron's truck pull to the curb, and minutes later there was a knock on the door. Aaron arrived with a bouquet of flowers in his hands. Miniature sunflowers and white and burgundy mums gave it an autumnal feel. "Aaron, they're lovely."

"You're making me dinner. It's the least I could do."

She hung his leather jacket in the closet by the front door, enjoying the leathery scent. When she returned to the living room, she found him sniffing the air too. "That smells amazing."

"It's spaghetti and tomato sauce. It's all vegetarian tonight. I hope you don't mind."

"I have no objections to eating something that smells so wonderful."

"Good. My sauce is kind of legendary. Tomatoes, onions, peppers, mushrooms, zucchini, and fresh herbs," she bragged. "Let me get the water boiling."

Aaron accepted a glass of water while he waited for her to get the pasta started.

Once dinner was on the table, conversation flowed easily. From the kids' homecoming plans to custody visitations to the struggles of single parenthood, they seemed to be in agreement on all the big stuff. Brooke had good girl-friends, but it was nice to have someone who understood that part of her world.

"What are your plans for Halloween?" Aaron asked after the plates were tucked in the dishwasher and they were relaxing on the sofa.

She shrugged. Jordan had stopped trick-or-treating before she went to high school, and they didn't have many children through her apartment building. "I really don't have any. I might get myself some candy to eat while I'm watching whatever PG horror movie they're playing on television, but that's about it."

"Would you like to do something with me instead?"

"Not the corn maze again?" she asked suspiciously.

"No."

"Good, because that is off the table. Is it a haunted house?"

"No."

"Stroll through a cemetery after dark? Ghost story competition? A trip to the local shelter to adopt a werewolf?"

"Darn, you got me with the last one," Aaron said with a laugh. "Where are you coming up with this stuff?"

"I told you. I have a highly honed Halloween spooky meter." It wasn't that she hated the holiday; she was just a big chicken who hated to be truly scared. "If it's none of those, what did you have in mind?"

"Unfortunately, I have the late shift on the thirty-first. I thought you might be interested in the early bird trick-or-treater's breakfast special at American Table that day. We can eat before you start at the hotel."

Of all the restaurants in town, American Table made the most menu changes for the holidays. Green pancakes on St. Patrick's Day. Red, white, and blue shakes for the fourth of July. For Halloween, they had jack-o'-lantern hash browns and pumpkin turnovers at breakfast. "That sounds good, but Halloween isn't for an entire month yet."

"I want to know I'm on your calendar well in advance."

She grinned. "That's not in question."

"Excellent. Then how about pencilling me in for another day?"

"Sure. Which one?" Brooke asked. She'd take any time with Aaron that she could get.

"A week Saturday night. It's my birthday party."

"I'm there!"

"It's a costume party," Aaron continued. "Since I usually work on Halloween, I always wanted a chance to dress up myself and to see Trevor's costume when he was a kid. It worked out well since he'd get to wear his outfit twice. Now it's tradition."

"I don't have a costume." A week wasn't very long to find something. The stores with the good stuff tended to sell out as soon as it hit the shelves, even this early before the big event, but she wasn't about to turn down being Aaron's date at his own birthday party. "I'm still in, though. Let me know when and where."

Sadly, she had homework left that needed to be done, and Aaron had his own obligations at home. She kissed him goodbye at the door, and once more when he stepped into the hall, loath to see him go.

"I could finish my rates of return homework another night."

"Don't worry, we'll have lots of nights once you're done."

"I must tell you that you're much more interesting than homework."

CHAPTER 11

THE LAST SATURDAY of September dawned with a glorious burst of orange. Brooke saw it from the east-facing second story hotel room of the Dew Drop Inn. She bundled the used linens into the laundry bag and snapped a fresh sheet open over the king-size mattress. Thankfully she only had three rooms to clean that morning. It was a dead period for the hotel: no weddings, no tourists, and no holidays where they had to take the overflow of families visiting locals. She'd be able to get through a majority of her work by ten thirty, hand off the common areas, change, and meet Aaron at By the Cup for a sandwich before her real work for the day—managing Corn Maze Night—started.

Her friend was waiting downstairs in dark slacks, a white shirt, and clean but worn work boots. "Lucy Callahan, reporting for mop duty." A small gold shamrock sparkled at the bottom of the chain that hung around her neck. Her honey-brown hair was pulled back with a headband, and she wore less makeup than she usually did, which let her summer tan shine through.

"Thanks, Lucy. I really appreciate this."

"No problem. What do you need me to do?"

She gave Lucy a list of the places that needed to be mopped, vacuumed, and dusted, then rushed home. Half an hour later, she stepped into the coffee shop and saw that Aaron already had a table. She'd hesitated at home, thinking she'd be overdressed in her long-sleeved turtleneck, orange and black plaid overshirt, jeans, and thick socks. That thought vanished quickly. Aaron had also layered his clothing, with a T-shirt under his police academy hoodie, and well-worn khakis which had faded to white threads where his wallet pressed against his back pocket.

Brooke waved, and pointed at the counter. She ended up face to face with the most talented barista in the place.

"Good afternoon, ma'am. What can I get you?" Jordan asked with a hesitant smile on her face.

Brooke glanced down the counter. Rachel Best, the owner, was doing her best to keep an eye on the situation without being obvious about it. "A large PSL in a to-go cup, a ham and cheese ciabatta, and a chocolate cake pop, please."

Jordan nodded in thanks when she realized her mother was going to act like a regular customer and not her mom. She carefully punched the order into the pad, then said, "We'll call you when your order is up. Thanks for visiting By the Cup today."

Brooke hesitated to give her time to continue, then gently prodded her daughter. "How much do I owe you?"

"Nothing. Your date already took care of it."

Jordan didn't look her in the eye when she dropped that bomb. "Excuse me?" Brooke asked.

Now her daughter had a full-on grin. "Sheriff Gillespie gave us more than enough to cover whatever you ordered and told us to use the rest as a tip. We'll call you when it's ready."

She couldn't argue and cause a scene when Rachel was hovering in case Jordan needed help, but it would definitely call for some payback for Aaron. For now, she'd play along. "Thank you for lunch."

"You're welcome."

The scent of pure black coffee escaped from his cup. "I'll be back for their dark roast as soon as pumpkin spice season is over," she said as she settled into the chair he'd saved her.

"Then will you switch over to an eggnog latte or something?"

"No, I'm loyal to pumpkin spice lattes and only them," Brooke told him. "Aside from that, it's dark roast with milk and no sugar."

"That's good to know. It'll make future orders easier."

"How about you?"

"Eggnog lattes are a must in December."

Her pressed sandwich was hand-delivered to her table, along with Aaron's roast beef on white. Knowing they didn't have much time if they were supposed to be at the Jackson farm by noon, Brooke dove into her meal.

"This isn't really a date since we have business to discuss, but I'm glad we have a little time together. How was your class on Monday?"

"Tough. We're learning interest rate calculations for investments and mortgages this week. Did you know they aren't done the same way?" Jordan had been sympathetic as Brooke sat at the other end of the island with her textbooks and calculator, muttering insults to the textbook's author. "But I'm a quarter of the way through the course already. I can do it." As hard as it was, her brain liked the work, once she understood the math. This was something she was good at, something that could support her and her family.

"You've got this," Aaron said.

"I do. Especially on Mondays and Tuesdays. Today, however, is for sunny fall days and adventurers." Brooke set down her coffee cup and waited until she had his full attention. "To be very clear, I will not be entering the maze today. No jokes, no emergencies, no way. I am the chief organizer and boss cleaner-upper. If somebody gets lost in there, they'll have to wait for the Monday search party like everybody else."

Brooke knew her phobia of cornfields at night was irrational. It didn't mean it wasn't real, though. She'd conquered her fear once, with Aaron, during the day. That was enough being brave for the time being.

He must have recognized her serious face. "Okay, no goofing around. You watch the outside, and I'll patrol the inside."

"You're actually going to do the maze?"

"I have a flashlight and backup batteries for after it gets dark. I'm going to alternate the right-turn plan with the left-turn plan and see which is faster. I figure I'll get through about six times."

She gasped. "That's got to be close to twenty miles."

"I'm wearing my hiking boots. You keep sending them in, I'll make sure people get out, and Trevor and Jordan will have an amazing fundraiser."

They ate quickly, then Brooke followed Aaron to the corn maze. The Jacksons had added more Halloween decorations since their last visit. Now costumed scarecrows guarded the entrance and exit. Brooke assumed there were more scattered throughout the maze and was grateful she'd already made her position clear. There was a short line at the ticket booth as people waited for the clock to strike noon.

Glenna came over to unlock the door and get her set up. "Sorry I'm late. We lost a kid over at the petting zoo by the pumpkin patch."

"Already?" Brooke teased. That's all she managed to say before the window opened, and people demanded arm bands, ready to begin their afternoon adventure.

There was a steady stream of customers from the moment they opened gates. The early birds were mostly families with young children looking for an afternoon's entertainment. After the first two hours, another parent replaced Brooke in the ticket booth, allowing her to wander and check in with all the other volunteers.

Brooke watched the exit for a while and wasn't surprised to see the children who led the way being carried out by the end. There were surprisingly few tears, and the couple meltdowns she did see vanished as soon as the popcorn stand came into view.

True to his word, Aaron waved goodbye as he stepped into the maze. He reappeared at the other end fifty-five minutes later with a limping woman leaning heavily on his arm and a tween who made a mad dash to the toilets.

"What happened?" she asked.

"Twisted ankle about ten minutes from the exit."

"Let's hope that's the only serious event of the day."

She wished. Aaron reentered the maze, then appeared around the corner twenty minutes later leading a man carrying a screaming two-year-old. The pair headed straight for their car, and Aaron came directly to her, begging for aspirin.

"What was that?"

"A temper tantrum of Godzilla proportions. That kid does *not* like corn."

"I don't blame him. Where did you come from?"

"We cut across some rows and came out on the east side of the field and walked back around. It was the fastest way."

"Any damage to the maze?"

"No. We were careful and took advantage of some natural gaps." He drained the water bottle she'd given him with the headache medicine she kept in her purse. "Are we almost done?"

"Not even close," Brooke told him.

By the time Jordan and two of her friends arrived at five, Brooke was ready for a break. She grabbed a popcorn and cola and found an empty bench near a firepit. When she and Aaron had last been there, the pits didn't get lit till after dark. Now they crackled merrily in the cool afternoon.

It didn't take Aaron long to join her. He stuck his legs out straight and flexed his feet. Little pieces of straw fell to the ground. "How much longer?" he asked.

"Four more hours for ticket sales. Five till the last of the stragglers should be out. Five and a half before we should be headed home." It was going to be a long day. Brooke didn't know if this was a regular Saturday at the corn maze, or if extra people were coming out to support the high school. Either way, the line hadn't grown any shorter no matter how many wristbands they'd issued.

Glenna came over. Brooke scooted down the bench to make room for her. "Is it always this busy?" she asked the owner.

"Yes, and it only gets busier the closer we get to

Halloween. We learned a few years ago this was the best weekend for the fundraiser. Lots of families, and fewer rowdy party groups after dark."

"Do you do bachelor and bachelorette parties?" Aaron asked.

"No," Glenna said. "We considered it, but there's usually alcohol involved in those. That's a liability we don't need. We get a lot of birthday parties for all ages, though." She looked at the people lingering in the rest area, and at the parking spots filling as soon as the last car pulled out. "We've got a good turnout for you. I hope everybody's having fun."

"I'm enjoying working out here in the open," Brooke said. "Aaron, on the other hand, has done the maze three times so far?"

"Four and a half," he corrected. "I figure I have time for one more while there's still a little daylight. Then I'll do it once more after you stop selling tickets."

"I'll join you for that one. You go right, I'll go left, and we should meet at the end," Glenna said. "In the meantime, I'm back to the pumpkin patch and petting zoo if you need me."

"Wait," Brooke exclaimed. "Did you find your missing kid?"

"I heard him, and William saw him, but he ran away before we could catch him. Don't worry, we'll get him."

Aaron leaned over and snagged a handful of popcorn. "I'm glad we didn't try to count this as a date. I've barely seen you this afternoon."

"Speaking of our date, what are you doing next Wednesday evening?" She had an idea.

"Nothing."

"Would you like to go out with me to Paint Night at the Starlight Gallery?"

About a year ago, Mina Blackburn put on one event a month at the gallery to get people to explore their artistic side. Normally, Brooke wouldn't have been able to afford them. Those classes were, and were priced as, a very nice date night activity. She hadn't wanted to miss out on it because money was an issue, so she approached her friend with a proposition. She gave the gallery and stained glass studio a thorough cleaning once a week, and she received two free passes to each class.

The Christmas stained glass classes in November and December were for her and Jordan, but Brooke had told Mina the two spots in the October session would be for her and Aaron. It was the first time she was bringing a date instead of a friend.

To her surprise, Aaron looked nervous. "I don't know what that is. Or how to paint."

"That's the fun of it. Mina has a sample painting and shows everyone how to do it. We each end up with our own version of the same picture." She tugged on his arm. "Come on, it'll be fun. Say yes."

"If we survive today, I'll do it," he said.

She cut him off before he could backtrack. "Great!"

"Mom!" Jordan yelled from the ticket booth.

"Break's over," Brooke said. Aaron squeezed her hand before he left to do another pass through the maze. She gave herself a moment to enjoy the feeling. The ten minutes she'd sat with him had revitalized her for the rest of the afternoon.

The last of the families left around five-thirty, offering a lull to grab a bite to eat at the popcorn stand or one of the food trucks before the evening. Then came the teenagers and the adults.

A breeze sprang up in the falling darkness. Blinding spotlights around the perimeter of the maze lit the central space well, but once people left those areas, they were on their own. Several of the groups carried flashlights. The less prepared pulled out their phones; Brooke wished them good luck and a long battery life before they headed in.

The popcorn booth and Fry Guys truck did brisk business, and all the tables were full of people and laughter.

A rush of cars arrived ten minutes before the ticket booth closed at eight, and several groups entered the corn maze one after another. Brooke had been keeping unofficial track of when groups entered and exited; it took significantly longer in the dark. Her hopes of getting away at their estimated time quickly dissolved when she realized it would likely take the final groups longer than the normal hour they allowed.

But her job was done. Brooke hung the Closed sign in the window and blocked the little cavity at the bottom of the plexiglass screen. Glenna arrived to help her count the evening's take, then left with the cashbox, leaving Brooke on her own.

Brooke wasn't in the mood for more popcorn or a hot dog and fries. There wasn't room around one of the firepits, and she didn't recognize anybody there anyway. Since she no longer had to keep an eye on the ticket booth, she took the opportunity to stretch her legs and began walking the length of the maze.

Bursts of laughter floated over the brown stalks that towered above her head. She heard some snatches of conversation, but most were erased by the scratching when the corn leaves rubbed against each other whenever the breeze picked up. Most of the noise came from far inside the maze.

Except for that bit of rustling. It was more than wind rocking the stalks; she saw the top of one plant bend and hold for second before swaying back to its normal position. Brooke paused, and the motion stopped. She took two more steps, then stopped again when the noise followed her.

She was under the spotlight in the corner, which meant the light from it spilled forward into the maze, not down around the perimeter. She was as far from the rest area and parking lot as she could get, which meant she wasn't getting any light from those areas either. "Who's there?"

The top of one stalk wavered. Then the one in front of it, closest to her. Brooke retreated a step. "This isn't an emergency exit, but if you need out of the maze, you're almost there."

A car turned out of the parking lot. For a brief second, the headlights cut across the corn row, illuminating a form that was about knee-high. The light continued to sweep sideways, and all of a sudden, two creepy white orbs shone brightly in the darkness. Then they moved closer.

"Aaaah!" Brooke yelled.

"Mah-ah-ah," the creature in the corn screamed back.

"Aaaah!" she yelled again as she stumbled backward.

The glowing eyes crept closer.

Suddenly there was movement behind her. "Brooke?"

"Aaaah! Help!" she screamed. She was surrounded.

"Brooke, it's me. It's Aaron." A warm hand gripped her forearm.

"There's a monster in there," she whispered. All of a sudden, she'd gone from screaming to barely being able to speak. She didn't want to draw its attention.

"Mah-ah-ah!"

Aaron pulled her back and shoved her behind him. His hand dropped to his hip, where he unclipped the huge flashlight that hung from his belt.

"Step out and identify yourself," he ordered loudly.

"Mah-ah-ah."

One of the creepy white eyes disappeared briefly but came back with a vengeance a moment later when the creature's head pushed through the last row of corn stalks. Black hair, white horns, white teeth. And a red collar. "Mah-ah-ah," the small goat called again.

"Penny?" a woman's voice called from behind them.

Brooke held onto Aaron, who held onto his flashlight, and they both stared at the little animal in front of them. "Brooke, it's a goat," he said. He may have said it twice. She wasn't certain over the blood roaring in her ears.

Then he laughed. "Brooke, it's okay. You can let go of my arm. It's a goat." He put away his flashlight so he could pull her fingers off his arm. "You're safe. No monsters. Let's get back to the rest area where there's better light."

Glenna pushed past them with a length of chain in her hands. "Come here, you rotten kid."

Brooke looked over her shoulder as Aaron led them away and saw the farmer threading the chain into the collar. "I don't understand."

"Glenna's goat escaped. Remember, she told us earlier that she was looking for her missing kid."

Brooke was sitting with a cup of hot chocolate in her trembling hands before she knew it. "I thought she was talking about her son, about Eli," she wailed. A tear slipped out of the corner of her eye. She was starting to see the humor in the situation, but a minute ago she'd been scared out of her mind. "That's not fair." She tried to laugh, but it turned into a hiccup.

"The normal expression is that when you hear hoof-beats, think horses, not zebras. With you, I think it should be when you hear bleating, think goats, not chupacabras."

She heard the humor in Aaron's voice, but couldn't quite match it. She realized she didn't need to when he crouched down in front of her. He draped a forearm over each knee. "Are you okay? I know you were truly spooked. You already hated the idea of a corn maze at night. You know nobody did this on purpose, right? It was a horrible coincidence that happened to the worst possible person." He rubbed his hands up and down her thighs. The heat from his palms stopped her legs from shaking.

"I know. I still feel like an idiot."

"Considering that half the people here screamed after you did, and they didn't see those otherworldly white eyes staring at them from the corn field, I wouldn't worry too much. Anybody in the maze will think that somebody screamed for effect. I wouldn't be surprised if Glenna got some extra-good reviews after this for the sound effects she added for atmosphere."

She managed a small snicker as he made air-quotes around "atmosphere." "I still feel like an idiot for freaking out."

"Next time you're accosted by a goat in the dark, you'll know what it is. How many people can say the same?"

That she laughed at.

Aaron stood. "I'm supposed to head in for my final sweep of the night. Are you going to be okay out here?" he asked.

"I'll be fine. I'll stay by the fires. Lots of people and lights. No goats."

Aaron bent and dropped a quick kiss on her forehead. "I'll be fast. Then I'll follow you home and make sure you get inside okay."

She was going to say that Jordan was here so she wouldn't be travelling alone, but she held her tongue. She wanted Aaron to follow her home and walk her to her door and kiss her goodbye after wishing her good night. It had been a long time since someone had taken care of her like that. She liked it.

CHAPTER 12

"TREV, DO YOU HAVE ANY QUARTERS?" Aaron asked as he rummaged through the coins on top of his dresser. Brooke had texted him asking if he had any loose change that she could buy off him. Apparently, her roll of quarters had gone missing, and she had plans to do her laundry that night. He hadn't seen her in a week. They texted constantly, and video chatted almost every day. He wished their schedules were more compatible, but he'd take what he could get.

"How many?"

"A couple dollars' worth if you've got it."

His son appeared at his bedroom door with a fistful of silver, which Aaron replaced with folded bills. "Did you have a chance to check out that link I sent you?" The teenager looked at him hopefully.

"I was going to ask you about that. Woodlands Trades Institute? Why are you looking at a trade school? What happened to U of M or St. Cloud?" Aaron asked, referring to the state's two largest colleges. When Trevor scratched the back of his neck, Aaron realized Brooke's laundry troubles would have to wait. "Why don't we have a seat in the kitchen?" he suggested.

He set a can of ginger ale in front of his son and pulled a cola for himself. "What programs are you looking at there?" He hoped to hear about plans for law enforcement, or maybe medicine if Trevor was inspired by his mother's side of the family.

"Woodworking. Cabinet making. Furniture," Trevor said quietly.

Aaron nodded, taking in the new information while trying to not to voice his first reaction, which was disappointment. "You haven't mentioned an interest in that before."

"Dad, you know I take shop every year. It's my favorite class. I told you I was working on an extra-credit project this semester with the wood I got from Mac's property. Mr. Schuler says it's going to be the best thing to come out of his workshop in the last decade."

If Aaron thought about it, he did know shop was his son's favorite class, and the one where he got the best marks. He had assumed it was simply because it was more fun that math or coding.

"The microwave stand you built last year is better than anything we could buy in a store," he admitted. Aside from giving Trevor the funds for supplies, he hadn't thought about it again until Trevor asked that he pick him up at school. The two of them had lifted the piece into the back of the pickup, and the shop teacher had raved about how well Trevor had done. Joints and biscuit cuts and other terms that had Trevor beaming. "Are you sure that is something you want to do as a career? Woodworking is a fine hobby—"

"It's not a hobby. It's a solid job." His son immediately went on the defensive.

"I'm not saying no. I'm saying I don't know much about it. What does your mother think?" That was a dodge and a weak attempt to avoid responsibility. He felt bad even as he said it because he knew the answer before he even finished the question. His ex-wife would throw a fit at the thought of their son doing manual labor. She'd never adjusted to Aaron being a police officer; while she liked the uniform, the rest of the job had been too hard for her. She'd been against Trevor following his father's career path. Heading into the trades would light a fire under her volatile temper.

"I was hoping to have you in my corner when I told her."

"And an acceptance letter already in your hand?" Aaron guessed.

"It wouldn't hurt," his son admitted. He wasn't wrong.

"I guess we'll be planning a campus visit, then."

The shock on Trevor's face caused a small pain in his chest. He hated to think his son expected such a big fight over his future. "Send me that link again, and I'll set it up."

"Thanks, Dad!" Trevor exclaimed before bolting to his room.

"Trev, I'm heading out for bit. I'll be right back," Aaron shouted at his back.

"Say hi to Ms. Portman for me."

"Smart aleck," Aaron muttered under his breath. But he was glad his son seemed okay with his father seeing someone new.

He dumped the coins into a baggie, then headed

across town. He didn't want to derail Brooke's study night with a long conversation about his son's future, but he'd at least get to see her for a couple minutes while he handed over her laundry money. She was waiting for him on the front step, wearing a thick hoodie and rubbing her hands together to ward off the chill in the evening air.

She waved a ten-dollar bill. "You can keep the change if you actually do the laundry for me. Washing and drying. I'll pay you extra if you fold it," she said with a smile.

"You'll have to add a zero to that bribe. I don't even fold my own laundry." He sat beside her. "Why are you sitting out here in the cold?"

"Is it cold? I'm in too much shock to notice." She sighed. "My darling daughter asked for permission to increase her number of shifts so she can save more money because she has her eye set on a couple of Ivy League colleges with journalism programs. The application fees are outrageous, never mind the tuition." Brooke blew a raspberry. "I don't want to tell her to aim lower, but the fees for out-of-state schools are so far beyond me. She'll be paying back student loans till she's fifty."

"That's not a problem for me. Trevor just informed me he wants to go to trade school for woodworking. He's not interested in college."

Brooke sighed again. "Kids, man. What are you going to do? Lock them in their rooms till they're thirty?" She looked at him hopefully. "That'll keep them from growing up, right?"

"Nah," he said. "It's too late for that. They already know how to open the windows."

"Shoot. It was so much easier when bribes were

yogurt tubes, and punishment was cutting off the Wi-Fi," she groaned.

Aaron chuckled. Trust Brooke to make him feel better when his teenager left him reeling. "If it makes you feel any better, tell Jordan to do the folding."

She beamed. "I will."

"How's the homework coming along?"

"I miss interest calculations."

"You said you hated interest calculations."

Brooke placed her hand on his knee and squeezed gently. "I was wrong, Aaron. So very wrong. I said that before I learned about depreciation scales. Now I love interest."

He smiled, because everyone had days like that. Most didn't involve math, but he understood the sentiment. He covered her small hand with his own. "You poor thing."

"Right? Totally. You'll have to be extra nice to me tomorrow."

"At Paint Night?" he asked. He still wasn't completely sure what that would entail. Roy had laughed at him when he'd mentioned it, then said, choking on his own words, that it hadn't been too bad. "I'm looking forward to it. I promise there will be no depreciation talk. Although you might want some by then."

"I doubt it, but I'll never say never." Brooke rose to her feet. "Thanks for the emergency quarters. I need to get back inside. My study group chat will be starting soon."

"Thanks for the laughs. I needed them." Trevor's news was still shocking, but it wasn't as horrible as he'd first thought. "I'll see you tomorrow."

"I'll be waiting."

CHAPTER 13

TWO PIECES of cloth fluttered like semaphore flags as Brooke held one shirt in front of her and then replaced it with another. "Do I want the red or the blue?"

"Blue," Jordan said.

"Okay."

"Speaking of okay, are you good with me and Aaron officially dating? We haven't really talked about it."

"Duh, Mom. You've been dancing around it for, like, a month already. Trevor and I think you two might be the only ones in town who don't know it's official. If I had a problem, you know I would have said something before now."

"That's true." Teaching her daughter to be vocal had its downsides on occasion. She was glad this wasn't one of them. "So, blue?"

"If you want to match. Like those old couples on the internet who always wear the same colors."

"What are you talking about?" She was more concerned about the old remark than she was about matching.

"Sheriff Gillespie. He almost always wears blue. It'll be like you coordinated in advance. It'll be cute."

Brooke threw the blue shirt onto the bed. "Red it is, then."

"What are you doing tonight? Dinner out? Oh, is he taking you to Colombo's? I know you love your Italian."

"No, we're doing Paint Night at the Starlight Gallery."

"Very cool. Are you going to trade paintings when you're done?" Jordan asked.

Brooke paused. "Is that a thing?" She'd hung her own paintings in her bedroom from two previous girls' night out experiences. The cherry blossom tree on a hill, and the wheat field at sunset weren't going to be displayed on a collector's wall anytime soon, but she'd been impressed with herself by the time she was done.

"It's a souvenir from your date."

She liked that idea. "I'll ask Aaron."

"Do it soon because he's here."

"I'll be home by ten," Brooke said. "You mentioned homework?"

"I have to keep those grades up to get my extra shifts."

Brooke tugged the red shirt over her head. She'd already done her hair and makeup, a little fancier than usual, since she'd only had one real chance to look good for Aaron, and the corn maze was a disaster she wanted to make up for. She thought she was doing pretty well, and her hair cooperated by not exploding into a staticky frizz-ball.

"Have fun!" Jordan shouted as Brooke skipped out the door.

Aaron was waiting outside his truck and offered her a hand as she hopped into the cab. "They've finished hanging the Halloween decorations on Main Street, and we have time. Do you want to see them before we go to the art gallery?" he asked.

"Definitely."

Most towns decorated their downtown for Christmas. A few did it for Independence Day as well. What Brooke loved about Holiday Beach was that they celebrated holidays all year round. The Chamber of Commerce had turned Holiday Beach's name into a marketing opportunity, and now all the businesses, and several neighborhoods, got in on the celebrations.

Halloween was lots of fun. Paper jack-o'-lanterns stared out from storefronts and would be replaced by fresh pumpkin faces later in the month. Little ghosts hung from light poles and floated in the breeze. Silhouettes of back cats lurked in corners of door windows.

That didn't include the costumes. Business owners ran the gamut from nothing at all to fully decked out for the season with makeup and prostheses and costumes that would put Hollywood to shame. Brooke didn't know how this year was going to play out at the Dew Drop Inn since it was now under new management. In the years she'd been there, the hotel had stuck to a ceramic jack-o'-lantern on the check-in desk and had banned costumes among the staff. They hadn't even participated in the safe trick-or-treat program where businesses gave candy to little boos and ghouls in the afternoon, so they didn't have to go out after dark.

"Does the police station do any holiday decorating?" Brooke asked. She'd never been inside the building, and she didn't remember ever seeing anything on the outside either.

"Not really."

"Would you like one? I didn't know this, but Jordan was telling me it's customary for people who participate in Paint Night to exchange pictures. You take my painting of whatever fall theme Mina has chosen, and I'll take yours. We can display them for the month of October."

His grin said he approved of the idea. "Deal."

The street in front of the Starlight Gallery was full of cars, so they parked a block away. Brooke was surprised to see all the seats filled but two. "We aren't late, are we?"

"We're right on time."

Mina greeted them and ushered them to the two empty chairs at the end of one of the four folding tables she'd scattered around the room. They joined Josh Huntington and his date, and Charlie and Josie Franklin. Each table had six small wooden easels, six blank white canvases, six jars holding a variety of paint brushes, and six plastic glasses half-filled with water.

"Aren't you all a bunch of eager artists?" Mina said loudly, drawing everyone's attention. Her dark hair and leopard print sweater suited their surroundings of colorful paintings and pottery. The black and orange polka-dotted cat ears on her head band were a nod to the holiday of the month. "I think you all know me, but in case you don't, my name is Mina Blackburn, and I own the Starlight Gallery. I'm thrilled to welcome you to our October art night. This month we will be making..." She paused for effect, then drew a white cloth off an easel. "A scarecrow at sunrise."

It was a happy, inoffensive design of a yellow scarecrow wearing blue overalls. It sat on a brown pole in front of a brown fence, and the sun was rising in the corner over a green field.

"I can't do that!" Aaron exclaimed. "Especially not in two hours."

"You can," Brooke assured him. "Just wait."

"You might want to start with your drink," Josh said, indicating the complimentary glass of wine Mina provided for each participant.

The tension eased from his face as Mina explained what was going to happen. They each took a wide brush from their jar and began wetting the canvas as instructed.

Mina came over to the table holding half a dozen paper plates with six colored blobs on them. "Are these all the colors we get?" Aaron asked.

"Red, yellow, blue, green, brown, and white are more than enough for this painting," Mina assured him. "Trust me."

Brooke nudged his shoulder with hers. "Relax. This'll be fun, I promise."

Aaron gave her an indulgent look, took another gulp from his wineglass, then waited for instruction.

Mina talked them through the background first. Aaron's horizon was as flat as a prairie landscape. Brooke's looked like she was painting the side of a hill. When Mina came around, she assured her that painting the scarecrow over it would even it out. The worried stress lines on Aaron's face were gone by the time he dipped his brush in the yellow paint for the first time and began painting his sun in the corner of the canvas.

They took a break after the first hour, letting their backgrounds dry and taking the opportunity to stretch and wander around the gallery. The door to Samuel French's stained glass studio was locked, but he had left a half-finished piece on display on his workbench. The overhead light spotlighted most of a Tiffany-style lamp shade.

Brooke pointed at it. "Art," she said. Then she pointed at her own painting. "Not art."

"Don't be discouraged. You still have the whole scarecrow to do," Aaron said.

She appreciated the encouragement. "Yours looks great already."

"I'm having a really good time. Especially since I've never done this before."

Jean and Gene Wyatt, a white-haired couple sitting at another table, called them over to chat. "She's in my study group and she's very helpful, so be nice," Brooke whispered.

"How's it going?" Jean asked.

"My painting works in the sense that it will scare birds away. I almost wish I was calculating depreciation," Brooke replied.

The men laughed. "Have fun with it," Gene advised. "This style is my forte."

"How so?" Aaron asked.

"All I can draw is stick people, so a scarecrow is perfect for me," the senior replied with a laugh.

When they returned to their seats, it was time to start on the scarecrow. Brooke's round, scarecrow face was a little uneven, so she added some paint to correct it. Then it grew into an oval. "How do I fix this?" she asked Aaron.

"Put a hat on it?" he suggested. "Mina encouraged us to improvise." Meanwhile, his scarecrow had a perfectly shaped head, with bits of brown straw sticking out artfully.

"That'll teach me to bring Minnesota's Michelangelo with me to Paint Night," she muttered.

The boatman hat didn't add anything to the general look of her painting, but it hid the lopsided head. Brooke had to admit that her coveralls were well painted, and the hands and feet looked scarecrow-like. Even Gene at the next table complimented them.

"It's time to start the face," Mina announced from the head of the room. "I want you to mix some blue and brown together. It should turn blackish. Then add the eyes." She showed them where to place them on the face, and how to twist the brush to make a small circle. "Then the smile."

"That doesn't look so hard," Brooke said to Aaron.

First, she sneezed, and her brush swooped across the paper, leaving a single eyebrow. She painted an eye directly below it and was grateful to see it was in the correct place. The other eye was narrower than the first. "I think the eyebrow is throwing off the perspective," she said, mostly to herself.

Then she added a matching one.

"Oh, no."

Beside her, Aaron set down his brush "What's the ma — What did you do?" he exclaimed.

"It was an accident."

"That's a very angry scarecrow. Why did you make him so mad?"

"He's not mad. He's got character," she said in defense of her art.

"Those are definitely angry eyebrows," Aaron argued. Meanwhile, his scarecrow's eyes twinkled on the canvas with a white dot in the center. Somehow he'd even managed to give it laugh lines in the creases and make it look like it was smiling.

"It'll be fine once I paint his mouth," she insisted.

It was not fine.

Aaron made a noise that sounded like he was trying not to laugh.

"My hand shook. I can fix it," she said defensively. The small black curve on the canvas became a thick curl threatening to split his head in half. She dropped her brush into the water cup in disgust. "I suck at this."

Aaron went and got a fresh glass of wine for her. "I asked Mina what she could do to help. She gave me this. She also said that you should let your paint dry before you try to make any more fixes." He wrapped his arm around her shoulders. "I'm sorry you're getting frustrated. Were you having a good time at all?" he asked.

His concern was touching, which made her feel slightly ridiculous. "I was, and I am. It's silly to get so upset over something like..." She waved at her canvas. "I wanted you to have a nice painting in your office from me."

"Your painting is still coming to the office with me. I'll hang it with pride."

If he still intended to put it up, she wasn't going to give up on it. "There's still time to fix it."

Under Mina's direction, she was able to turn the wonky mouth into a stern smile. Then, before Mina cleared the paint from the table, Brooke copied Aaron's idea of adding a couple dots of white to the eyes to give them some depth and sparkle.

Charlie Franklin offered to take pictures of them with their paintings. Aaron held his proudly, while Brooke knew she wore a more rueful smile. Charlie gave them a thumbs-up, then gasped when he saw the photo on Aaron's phone screen. "It's watching me," he said.

"What is?" Aaron asked.

"Brooke's painting." He moved the phone back and forth, then handed it to Aaron. Then he looked at Brooke's canvas, took a couple steps to the left, and stared again. "Yep, those scarecrow eyes follow you."

"He's joking, right?" she asked Aaron.

"Of course he is."

She turned the painting around. The eyes were a bit weird, but they looked like scarecrow eyes as far as she was concerned. Brooke squinted. "The hat makes him look like a detective from the thirties. He's a Depression era private eye."

"He's going to be hanging in my office," Aaron said.

"That's cool," Charlie said. "As long as he won't be haunting one of my apartment buildings. I've got to get back to my wife. Enjoy your picture."

The evening breeze off the lake had gone from chilly to cold. Aaron laid the paintings faceup on the back seat. "That was fun, paint disaster notwithstanding. Thanks for doing it with me," Brooke said. It had been a long time since she'd done a strictly grown-up activity on a date. Girls' nights were fun, but it was nice having someone to dress up for. Especially someone who encouraged her when she made a mess and laughed with her when she threw up her hands and made the best of it.

"Thank you for suggesting it. Does Mina do one every month?"

"She does something."

"I'll have to keep that in mind in the future."

The ride home ended much too quickly. She could have hopped out when he pulled to the curb, but she lingered in the warm cab. Aaron had calmed her, and had brought her humiliation down to manageable levels, but she still didn't want to go into the apartment.

"So next time is my turn to pick something, right?" Aaron asked.

"Next time it is," she agreed.

"You'll have to give me a couple days to think of something. Not a Monday or Tuesday night, right?"

"Right." She hesitated. "I guess I should go."

Aaron reached across the console dividing their seats and caught her coat collar between his fingers. She let him pull her closer.

He kissed her gently on the lips, then let her go, even though she didn't want him to.

"Wave from the window when you get upstairs, okay?"

"Okay," she agreed breathlessly.

He was pulling away when she realized she'd left her painting in his truck.

CHAPTER 14

IT FELT like the opening to a horror movie. A low mist covered the ground, and the sunrise looked redder than normal, casting an eerie glow over everything. Then there was the dialogue. "Dad, it's watching me." Trevor glanced over his shoulder, then sat straight in his seat, eyes staring dead ahead.

"Throw my sweater over it." The dawn of a new day did nothing to improve Brooke's painting. If anything, the eyebrows looked even angrier now that he saw every brush stroke in the bright sunlight. "Next time you'll check to make sure your trunk is properly closed so the battery doesn't die."

"Trust me, I've learned that lesson. Are you really going to hang that in your office?"

"That was the deal," he said.

"You must like her."

"I do." Aaron glanced at his son while they were stopped at a red light. Every date they'd had had shown them to be more compatible than he'd originally thought.

That, and he was learning that Brooke was funnier and smarter than he'd ever imagined. He was picturing her being in the picture for a long time. "Are you okay with that?"

"Yeah. It's not like she's moving in next week. Is she?" There was a tone in Trevor's voice that sounded a little worried.

"No chance. We're just dating."

"I think Ms. Portman must like you too," Trevor said when they were moving again.

"How's that?"

"She made you something that will cause people to confess if they're in the same room with it for more than five minutes."

Aaron's eyes flickered to the rearview mirror. "I wonder if that would work. Do you have anything to confess?"

"I threw three of my socks in your laundry basket because I found them on the floor after I cleaned my room and I'd already done my laundry."

"I think we can let that slide. Nothing else?"

"Not that I'm willing to admit."

"Maybe I should hang Detective Hayseed in your locker," Aaron teased. "See what else you remember."

"Dad, if I opened my locker and found that thing in there, I'd confess to anything you wanted."

"I'll keep that in mind. I'll pick you up after school."

"It's okay. I want to talk to Mr. Schuler. I'll walk."

After dropping Trevor off at school, Aaron headed to work. The parking lot at the station was remarkably full for first thing in the morning. Excluding the staff's cars, Aaron counted three vehicles he recognized by sight. "This should be fun," he mumbled to himself as he strode to the door carrying Brooke's painting in one hand, his sweater still covering it.

Neil Dempsey was the first in line at the counter, and Aaron could hear him before he could see him. He was surprised to see Mac Mackenzie as one of the other people behind Neil.

"Neil, if you don't stop screaming at our receptionist, we're going to have words you will not enjoy." Aaron's voice was as cold, and he was not faking his displeasure. "That is unacceptable behavior, and you know it. Now, calmly and at a regular volume, tell me what's going on, starting with whether or not the three of you are here together or have different complaints."

"We are all here together to file a complaint against you for dereliction of duty and to demand an investigation into the robberies along Shakespeare Drive."

Aaron leaned over the counter. "Poppy, can you get me the reports from last week?" he asked the blonde-and-gray-haired administrative assistant. "Would you all like to discuss these here, or shall we move to an interview room?"

"The interview room would be great, Sheriff, thanks," Mac said before Neil started on another rant.

Aaron looked to the front door when it opened again. He was surprised to see Lucy Callahan. "Do you have a cottage on Shakespeare Drive too?" he asked. He hadn't heard anything about her buying property in town. According to Roy, she was happily settled into her new apartment in Brooke's building.

"No." She sounded as confused as he was.

"Can you wait while I deal with this other situation? Or can someone else help you?"

"I can wait."

With that problem solved for the moment, he waited for Poppy Zimmer to return with the file he requested before he entered the interview room. He set his painting on the chair, then turned to face the trio of Holiday Beach residents.

He knew two well: Robert "Mac" Mackenzie, and Neil Dempsey. Sean Fitzpatrick owned Austen Cottage, but he didn't visit Holiday Beach often.

"Am I to understand that you've all had break-ins?" Aaron asked.

"If you bothered to investigate when I complained to you last week, you'd know that we have," Neil said.

Poppy paused in the door and cleared her throat. The older woman had worked for the police department since before Aaron had joined the force. She knew everything that went on in Holiday Beach and was doubly respected in the community for keeping it all confidential. Rumors stopped dead in her presence. The woman was a Sphinx.

Aaron took the file from her, slapped it on the table, flipped through the forms, and pulled out a single sheet of paper. "Here's my report, filed after you accosted me in the Atlas. I investigated that night. I went to Austen Cottage. I did not find the glider swing covering on the property. I also inspected that building and found nothing amiss. I notified the owners of this by email, didn't I, Mr. Fitzpatrick?"

"You did, Sheriff Gillespie."

"Then, regarding the second part of your complaint, the next day I called Joe Piney to ask if he'd left the tires at the end of the driveway. He wasn't available, so I spoke to his son, Gerald, who said his nephew had left the tires there when they were out last to check the cottage before winter. When I told him they were missing, he said it wasn't a problem and that Joe Junior had put a free sign on them and was planning to have Tom's Tows take them to the recycling centre if they didn't go on their own. I also informed him that I'd made an exterior inspection of the cabin at that time and didn't find any sign of a break-in. He said it wasn't necessary for me to investigate further."

"I didn't know that," Neil said.

"So, you looked once and didn't find a stolen item, so you stopped looking? What kind of police work is that?" Neil demanded. He looked like he was building to another rant, so Aaron cut him off.

"Mac, I hadn't heard you were having problems," Aaron said, addressing the stocky, dark-haired man with more patience than he used in his recitation.

"Neil said some things might have gone missing from my property. I checked before I came here this morning. All my tools are still in the container, and the lock hadn't been tampered with."

"You told me some firewood had been stolen," Neil argued.

"I told you some wood had been taken. I also told you I'd given the sheriff's son permission to take whatever he wanted from particular areas. I didn't expect him to clear out the scrap pile, but I wasn't going to complain about it. It's less for me to get rid of later."

"So why are you here, Mac?" Aaron asked.

"If someone is breaking into cottages along Shake-speare Drive, I'd like to know about it. I haven't started building yet, but I'd like to keep an eye out for my neighbors," Mac said.

Now that Aaron knew the trouble was coming from one man, and that he hadn't brushed aside news of a crime spree because he was on a date, he found it easier to regain his professionalism. "Let's take a step back and look at this clearly. Right now, what we have is some scrap wood, assumed to be given away, free used tires taken with the owner's blessing and potentially some missing firewood," he added, remembering Neil's original complaint.

"And a tarp," Neil added.

"And a tarp. Mr. Dempsey, it's commendable that you're acting as a neighborhood watch, but nobody, including your wife, has reported anything stolen."

"What about my firewood? That's stuff's not cheap."

Although Aaron doubted Neil had bought a bag at the gas station when so much was lying around for free on his property, he wasn't going to debate it. "You're talking about five logs. That was according to your own state- ment. After last weekend, I feel it's a logical assumption that it might have been burned by a member of your family, even it if wasn't done at your cottage, wouldn't you say?" Neil had been livid when he'd arrived at the station in the wee hours last Sunday morning to bail out his son. Aaron had expected more yelling, but upon hearing the damage the party had caused, Neil had been suspiciously quiet. He'd made up for it today, but Aaron wasn't having any of it.

He tried not to smile when he saw Mac rolling his eyes at this latest revelation. "I don't have time for this," the painter said. "If there's a real problem, please let me know. As I said, I'll keep my eyes open. In the meantime, I have painting to do. Doug's waiting for me on a jobsite already."

Mac's words gave Aaron an idea. "Speaking of paint- ing, do you want to see the one Brooke made for me at

Paint Night last night? I'm going to hang it in my office." He set the painting on the table and dropped the sweater.

There was a collective hiss at the reveal. Aaron kept the canvas facing them. The initial response from Mac and Sean quickly jumped from interest to shock. Neil went straight to horror. "Isn't it terrific?" Aaron asked.

"It's...something," Mac said.

Aaron turned to face Neil, twisting the painting slightly so it moved with him. "Was there anything else you'd like to discuss this morning?"

"Um. No."

"If you do discover anything is missing, please let me know. We all know that empty cabins can be an opportunity for thieves."

"I'll, uh, do that," Neil stammered. "I need to go." He didn't take his eyes off the painting as he backed out of the room.

Aaron lay the canvas face down on the table. "I can't believe that worked."

"What is that thing?" Sean Fitzpatrick asked with a nervous laugh.

"That truly is a painting my girlfriend made for me. I am going to put it in my office," Aaron said.

"Brooke's great, but did you lose a bet?" Mac asked. "Because it was watching me."

"I'm calling him Detective Hayseed. My son says it's a confession extractor."

"He's right," Sean agreed.

"He's starting to grow on me," Aaron said loyally. No matter how it looked, he knew Brooke had worked hard on it for him. The gift was a treasure; the side effects were an unexpected benefit. Besides, if he hung it behind his desk, he wouldn't have to look at it when he was in his office. It would also ensure nobody overstayed their welcome.

"I think I need to go too," Mac said, slowly moving toward the door.

"Seriously, if either of you see something odd, or if you have problems, let me know. Neil isn't the most unbiassed witness in this case, but he's not wrong to be concerned."

"I will," Sean said before his escape.

Aaron was grateful the situation was resolved before it became a real problem. Now that it was resolved, he had a chance to address a second topic. "Mac, do you have a second? How has Trevor been working as your landscaping assistant?"

"Great. That kid of yours really likes wood. I had no idea when I asked him, but it's a bonus for me."

"Is he behaving properly? Not goofing off?"

"Not at all. He and Caleb work hard."

"Caleb?"

"Caleb Quentin. He's the other teen I hired. He works his butt off too. If Trevor came back and collected the rest of that scrap lumber, you'll have enough for bonfires all fall."

"We've already had one. Thanks for the update."

Mac shook his hand before he left, leaving Aaron with a good feeling about his son. Cutting down trees and building furniture wasn't the future he'd envisioned for Trevor, but his son seemed to enjoy it and work hard at it. Aaron couldn't ask for much more.

He grabbed his painting and headed for his office but stopped when he saw Lucy waiting in the lobby. "Come on in, Lucy."

Deciding he'd terrified enough people with his

painting for one morning, he set it on the floor before he settled behind his desk. "What's up with you?"

"I'm here as the manager of the Remington apartments. I have a problem."

He hadn't expected this. "Do you want coffee?"

"No, thanks."

"Then tell me what's happening."

Her tale got weirder by the minute. Aaron knew that Lucy had started her job managing the three apartment blocks in May, replacing the previous caretaker after his retirement. From all the comments he'd heard, from the residents and the Franklins, who owned the buildings, she'd been doing a good job keeping the place clean, repaired, and functional. Her experience as a property maintenance manager at the Dew Drop Inn's parent company had trained her to fix any number of problems. In less than five months, the Remington had gone from having vacancies to having a waiting list for their two-bedroom apartments.

"The Quentin family. The lease was signed by Priscilla and Arthur, and they had one child listed as a dependent."

"Caleb."

"Right," she said. "I hadn't seen the parents in months. Since August, maybe. Their rent has been paid. Their lease expired at the end of September. I never heard back on my inquiries on whether or not they wanted to renew it. I assumed it was a yes, but they were late on the paperwork. I thought I'd get a check on October first, but nobody answered the door. They have ten days before late fees kick in. I knocked on their door on the tenth and it sounded weird inside, echoey, so I let myself in. They're gone."

"Gone?"

"Not a stick of furniture. No clothes. Nothing in the fridge. I didn't hear a peep about them moving out."

"Was the place trashed? Will their damage deposit cover it?"

"It was relatively clean. My problem is that I don't know where to send the damage deposit. I've seen Caleb in passing around town, but I haven't had a chance to ask him."

"Moving without notice isn't a crime."

"I'm still concerned. Can you look into it? If only to find out where I should send their refund?" Lucy asked.

The joys of small-town life meant that the lack of severe felonies gave him more time to investigate misdemeanors and even non-criminal events. "Fine, I'll do it."

"Brooke's right. You are the best. After Roy, of course."

"She said that?"

"I probably shouldn't have mentioned it."

No, she definitely should have mentioned it. "It's fine. I'm happy to help." Maybe this favor wouldn't be such a hardship.

CHAPTER 15

AARON STARED at himself in the mirror. He ignored the sprinkling of white in his sandy brown hair at his temples and focused on the stitches across his throat. Trevor claimed to have a friend in the drama department who gave him tips on making fake wounds. Aaron's old black suit, already well-worn but now with additional artistic rips and stains, was the perfect choice to go with his formal Frankenstein's Monster look. The glued-on plugs at his neck sat above the frayed shirt collar so he didn't have to worry about them rubbing off. Beneath that, his tie looked like it had been half-eaten by a shredder. He was a mess and couldn't be more pleased about it.

His birthday present from Trevor had been an afternoon of fishing. Having his son sacrifice a Saturday afternoon with his friends to hang out with his old man had meant a lot. Then Trevor had surprised him with a specific trip to his favorite spot even though it was on the far side of the lake. They hadn't had any luck, but the point of fishing wasn't always to catch fish. Aaron heard more about Woodlands Trades Institute and its apprenticeship programs. Both of them bemoaned how hard it was to date at their respective ages, although Aaron got some grudging respect for actually having a girlfriend.

The rain started when they were packing up. It was coming down in buckets by the time they turned into their driveway, and the sky had turned from gray to nearly black.

Trevor had hung around long enough to sample the catering Aaron had delivered. There was a new business in town, Norah's Nosh, which had offered a deal to new clients that he couldn't turn down. Aaron was willing to try somebody new if it meant he didn't have to cook or clean up. So far, the sandwiches and dip were incredible. The cake, safely secured on the bottom shelf of his fridge, looked to be a delicious, gooey delight. He could have done without the little meringue ghost decorations, but Aaron knew this was the caterer's chance to show off to potential new customers, so he left them in place. Except for the one Trevor had peeled off the corner and popped into his mouth.

"Itch de lease you can do shinsh I'm not getting cate," the kid had said through a mouthful of meringue.

"I'll make sure I save you a piece. This thing is filling the whole shelf. There will be leftovers."

"Too late."

When Brooke volunteered to come over early and help set up, Aaron offered to pick her up. He'd never had a co-host at one of his parties, and he thought Brooke would be excellent at it. Besides, he was game for anything that would give them more time together. Her super-early mornings and his late nights at the station were putting a serious crimp in their time together. It made being together tonight more special.

She must have been waiting in the lobby, because she made it to the sidewalk before he had a chance to get out of the truck. Aaron burst into laughter when he saw her and was still chuckling when she climbed into the passenger seat.

"How did I do?"

"You're perfect."

She'd dressed as a scarecrow. Specifically, Detective Hayseed. She had a boatman's hat, which looked to be left over from a political rally a decade earlier, and wore a white shirt under a pair of blue overalls. Straw—"raffia," she told him—was sewn onto the collar and stuck on the underside of the hat. She'd sewn more at the cuffs at her wrists, and her shoes were completely covered from the flapping beige strands at her ankles. What really made the costume were the thick, angry, grease-paint eyebrows she'd angled over her eyes. They made Groucho Marx's look like amateur hour.

"Now I regret having that painting at the station. We could have had a picture of you painting a self-portrait." Some people wouldn't get the joke, but enough of the invited guests had seen it to make her costume extra funny.

"Your outfit is pretty good too. Are you ready for an onslaught of Frankenstein puns?"

"Technically, I'm the monster," Aaron said.

"I know. A smart person knows Frankenstein wasn't the monster. A really smart person understands Frankenstein was the monster," Brooke told him.

"That's pretty deep for a birthday party."

"I have hidden scarecrow depths."

They arrived back at Aaron's and immediately began prepping by placing bowls of chips strategically around the living room and dining room. He'd vacuumed under the cushions of the leather sectional and had tossed all the pillows and blankets into his bedroom for the night to maximize the space. The coffee tables were clear of flyers and magazines, and all the remotes for the electronics were in a basket on top of the shelving unit that housed the gaming consoles. Thanks to Trevor's cleaning spree in September, the kitchen was still in good shape. The bathroom—Aaron tried not to think of what had been required in the bathroom, but it was guest-ready now.

He wasn't surprised when the first to arrive were the ones who had children at home. Tripp Turner and Habibah Gamal arrived as soon as the restaurant closed. Their one-year-old was with Tripp's parents for the evening. Aaron was glad to see they were taking advantage of a night out.

"May the Force be with you," Aaron said in greeting. Habibah was in a full Stormtrooper uniform, a white scarf covering her hair and conveniently making it easier to put on and take off her helmet. Tripp looked like a bounty hunter who'd had seen better days, with his scuffed armor and bent laser rifle.

"We heard you had cookies," Tripp said.

"Tripp, we did not come to sample the competition," Habibah whispered.

"We didn't *only* come to sample the competition," Tripp corrected. "But we did want to celebrate our friend's birthday. Seeing the spread Norah Rail offers for a party is a bonus."

"We'll pull the trays out in a minute," Aaron promised. "In the meantime, the bar is on the dining room table."

Behind them was Owen Daye, who had only recently

arrived in Holiday Beach to take over his grandfather's antique store. Aaron had met him at a few events at the Escape Room, and they'd got along well enough for Aaron to invite the newcomer to his party so he could get to know more people in the community. Knowing Owen had a young son at home, Aaron asked, "I assume your little boy has the other half of your costume?" The thin blond man in the bandit's mask and striped shirt with a dollar sign on his chest was a dead giveaway to needing a partner in crime, so to speak.

"Richie is looking forward to Halloween and is very put out that I got to wear my costume first. Thankfully, Pops reminded him that he gets to wear his costume to daycare and to several parties, but I only get to wear mine to one. I also had to promise not to let the sheriff arrest me, because only Spidey was allowed to do that," Owen said with a laugh.

"Keep your hands off my silver candlesticks, and we won't have any problems," Aaron agreed.

Brooke brought him a drink before she said hello to Roy Wagner and Lucy Callahan, who came as a couple from the 1920s. Roy's dapper suit was well matched to Lucy's flapper dress.

Mina Blackburn was an awesome ninja turtle behind her half-shell and purple mask. Samuel French's beret and black shirt and slacks did give him the air of a Parisienne artist, but it wasn't far from his everyday look.

Josh Huntington, the owner of Holiday Beach's biggest gym, wore jungle camouflage and an uncomfortable looking pith helmet. Mac Mackenzie, who arrived at the same time as Josh, looked like Aaron pre-death. "Mr. Bond, I presume?" Aaron said to the house painter in the tuxedo and slicked back hair.

Aaron wandered the room, making sure everyone was fed and watered and having a good time. The sandwich and snack trays were a huge hit with everyone; he was sure Norah's Nosh would have more business in the future.

He wrapped his arm around Brooke's waist as he recounted their afternoon at the corn maze to some eager listeners. She turned a brilliant shade of red when he got to the point of her and the goat screaming at each other, but she was laughing too hard to tell him to stop.

Brooke leaned into his arm. "We should probably do the cake in the next fifteen minutes or so. Habibah and Tripp will have to leave soon," she said to him quietly.

The kitchen was empty, so Aaron took advantage. He pressed Brooke against the counter and kissed her. Brooke was still a little shy, and he didn't know if they were at the kissing level of public displays of affection yet, but everyone else was still out in the living room. "That's a birthday kiss. I'm totally allowed to do that."

"You sure are. I think we should make birthdays a weekly event," she agreed when she caught her breath. "Unfortunately, you still have a house full of guests."

"Grab the cake, and let's get them out of here."

He tried not to turn red when Brooke led the guests in a round of "Happy Birthday." She stuck a candle in his slice of chocolate and vanilla marble cake, and he had to let the wax drip while everyone else received their pieces before she let him make a wish and blow it out. His wish was simple: that his relationship with Brooke continue to move forward as well as it had so far.

It was closing in on midnight when the last of his guests finally departed. He gathered the paper plates and disposable bamboo cutlery and saved them for a fire in the backyard at a later date; Brooke took over putting away the food. They rearranged the furniture in the living room, so everything was back in its usual place. They had a cup of coffee to relax after all their work, but he couldn't come up with any more excuses after that to delay taking her home.

"Do you want to take the long way, down Shakespeare Drive?" he suggested. It had been the best birthday he'd had in ages, and he didn't want it to end.

"That is nowhere near my house."

"That's why it would be the long way."

She grinned. "Drive slowly."

CHAPTER 16

AFTER EIGHT HOURS, Brooke expected the storm to have blown itself out. If possible, it had exploded into more violence. Instead of rain, now there was lightning and gale force winds. The limbs of the spruces lining the road flapped wildly. The road following the shore of Star Lake was usually a leisurely drive that offered glimpses of moonlight reflecting off still water. Tonight, it looked like an endless, bottomless pool of black. "As much as I enjoy spending time with you, this isn't the most romantic drive we've ever taken, Aaron."

The truck rocked, and she saw his fingers tighten around the steering wheel until his knuckles were a stark white. "The weather station did not predict this. We need to get off the road."

It was too little, too late. Lightning struck a fraction of a second before a thunderous boom shook the truck. Sparks flew from a tree on the shoulder. Brooke didn't scream, but her intake of air was a squeak. Aaron swore and cranked the wheel hard. They swerved, narrowly avoiding the towering spruce falling toward them. Brooke gripped the dashboard with both hands as she braced to hit the ditch, but the truck bounced a couple times, then stayed level as Aaron pulled off the road. They rolled on for a few more seconds until he hit the brakes.

"Where did you turn? Where are we?" she asked, still gasping in shock.

"This is the driveway to Shelley's Shack." Aaron laid his hand on her shoulder and turned to look at her. "Are you okay?

Brooke took a deep breath, held it, then exhaled. "A little shaken up, but I'm not hurt. That was some good driving."

"Thanks, but we won't be going anywhere for a while." He gestured behind them.

The tree had not only fallen across the road, but it had also fallen lengthwise down the center of the drive-way. The rain and the puddles had put out any obvious flames from the lightning strike, but smoke and steam still sizzled from the scorched branches. There was another flash and simultaneous crack of thunder, which made her jump in her seat again.

"We should get out of the truck."

"If we're in the truck, the tires will keep us safe if we're hit by lightning. Mostly."

"But we're at risk for falling trees. I think we should make a run for it."

"And go where?" she demanded.

"I can force the cabin door open. I'll fix it and apologize to Joe Piney later. We don't have a choice. It's too dangerous to stay out here."

Brooke set her hat on the seat beside her, knowing it would probably melt if it got wet. She had her jacket, but no umbrella or hood. When they ran, she was going to get drenched, but wet and cold inside was safer than being trapped in a truck during a lightning storm. "I'm ready."

The sagging roof and missing siding pieces on the exterior indicated nobody had done any repair work on it in years. The cabin did have a covered porch, but it wasn't much use. The wind drove the rain in almost horizontally. Brooke's pant legs and shoes were soaked. She felt the cold rain run down her legs and pool around her toes. Aaron carefully broke the glass pane closest to the door's lock, reached through, and opened it from the inside.

They stepped onto a threadbare, rag-braid rug and dripped for a moment while Aaron closed the door. Brooke's fingers fumbled along the wall until she found a light switch, but the darkness remained. "The power's out, or shut off," she reported.

The room was filled with inky shadows. There wasn't any moonlight to shine through the narrow gaps in the curtains to give the barest illumination. Brooke fished her phone out of her pocket and activated the flashlight. The last time she'd been at Shelley's Shack, there hadn't been much to see. Entering through the front door instead of the back only showed the same mess from a different angle.

Three mismatched sofas created a U around the cold fireplace. Two pushed-together kitchen tables filled the other half of the large room. Brooke counted eight chairs around them, haphazardly placed, as if Aaron hadn't wasted time doing more that setting them back on their feet. A stove, fridge, and short counter lined the wall behind them. There were four doors on the far wall: three looked like they led to bedrooms and the fourth had a toilet beyond the door.

"Do you see the candles on the mantle?" Aaron asked.

"I put them back when we cleaned after taking the photos for the files."

She did see a collection of tealights on the mantle. Brooke toed off her shoes, then walked over to the fireplace on squishy socks. Aaron had thoughtfully placed a barbecue lighter and a pack of matches beside them. Soon the room was bathed in a yellow-orange glow which was reflected from the mirror set above the fireplace.

A loud crack of thunder made them both jump. "Is it ridiculous that I feel a little better being in a building instead of a car?" she asked.

Something crashed outside before Aaron had a chance to answer her. He reopened the door, looked on the porch, then closed the door again. "Not ridiculous at all. Also, the rain is no longer blowing in from the east side of the house."

"Why not?"

"A pine tree is blocking it. We're lucky it didn't take out part of the roof."

She started shaking again, and it had nothing to do with the chill in the air. "I hope Jordan is alright."

"Is she working?"

"No, she should have been home hours ago."

"Text her and tell her where you are and that it will be a while before you get home. I'll try to get a fire started so we can dry out."

Brooke typed a short text, then sighed in relief at her daughter's prompt response. "All's good at home. Do you need to text Trevor?"

"He's at his mom's. He's not expecting to hear from me tonight."

While Aaron made use of the basket of ads and flyers and stack of logs by the fire, Brooke took a candle and checked out the bathroom. The shelves above the toilet were empty except for two folded beach towels. She grabbed one for herself and shook it open. An orange-and-black striped tiger in a blue speedo greeted her. She grabbed the other for Aaron, then returned to the living room.

Flames flickered at the edges of the newspaper. She held her breath when a drop of water fell off the flue and spattered on a corner, putting out that flame, but the rest of the paper caught and was soon blazing. The paper burned quickly, but thankfully the log's bark glowed orange for a moment before tiny flames caught there too. "This will take the chill out of the air. We got lucky. We should have enough in this pile to get through the night. Anything I brought in from outside wouldn't dry for a week."

"I have towels. I feel bad that we're making ourselves right at home."

"We don't have another choice. It's this or being outside. The Pineys have always been decent people. They wouldn't want anyone to suffer when there was shelter available."

Brooke grabbed a couple chairs and set them next to the fire. She hung her jacket and socks over one, then moved it a foot to the left when she saw it was under a leak in the exposed roof. She dug a pot out of a kitchen cupboard and set it on the floor. Soon they were listening to drops hit the metal.

She curled up on the sofa, pulled an afghan off the back, then patted the cushion beside her. "Let's conserve body heat."

A flurry of sparks rose when Aaron gave the logs a poke. He waited a moment to make sure the logs were burning well before he joined her. "This is not how I expected my birthday party to end."

"Me either."

The fire looked hot, but it wasn't throwing off enough heat to warm the room. Brooke shivered and drew the afghan to her chin. Aaron shifted closer to her and wrapped his arm around her shoulders. "It'll be warm in here soon."

"Distract me. Have you ever had a cottage like this?"

"Owned, no. Borrowed, often. We used to take a vacation every summer when Trevor was little. Most of the time we'd get a week at Tara's family place on Lake Michigan." He chuckled. "We'd have to bribe Trevor to come out of the water at the end of the day, then check to see if he'd grown gills. How about you?"

"Once. Another military spouse and I rented a place on the Delaware coast while our husbands were away. It was about as nice as this place." Brooke chuckled, but it wasn't because her memories were funny. "The owner was a real piece of work. When we arrived, all of a sudden, a bunch of extra expenses popped up. An extra fee to connect the propane to the barbecue, which the other mom knew how to do. A rental charge for the water equipment, but fortunately we'd brought our own." She laughed again, and this time it was real. "The oven in the kitchen wasn't working. I called my dad, and he sent me to the hardware store and told me how to change the fuse. I replaced it, no problem. When we checked out, the owner tried to keep our damage deposit because we'd broken the stove."

"Which meant he knew it was broken when you arrived."

"Yep. We told him it wasn't broken, and he threw a fit,

but he couldn't say anything when he turned it on and it worked."

"Did you report him?"

"It was a private rental, but you can bet I made it my mission to ensure nobody on base ever rented from him again, and his online reviews took a sudden downturn." She snuggled deeper into Aaron's side.

"I'm sorry you had such a bad experience."

"It wasn't completely horrible. We were on the seashore, and the public beach nearby was amazing. I'd like to rent another place. A nice one, where everybody gets their own bedroom. Someplace with a dock and a deck and a firepit. Ooh, and a hot tub," she said dreamily.

"Private chef? On-call masseuse?" Aaron teased.

"Is that an option?"

"Sadly, not that I've seen."

Another flash lit the sky so brightly she saw it through the curtains. The thunder that followed shook the panes in their frames. "This storm is not letting up."

"We're safe and dry," Aaron added. "It's almost romantic. You, me, candles, a roaring fire. All we need is some wine and leftover birthday cake. I'm kicking myself for not packing a cooler."

"To be fair you didn't know we'd need supplies for the drive home." The heat from the fire had reached her feet, so she stretched them on the coffee table and enjoyed the warmth. The rain on the roof had stopped hammering down, then took a breath before starting again; it now fell in a hard but steady rhythm. The sound was almost soothing, especially when she heard it bouncing off the corrugated tin roof of the porch.

"This is ridiculous. I'm falling asleep," she said, snuggling even closer to Aaron. He was warm and safe and really comfy, like her own personal, life-size teddy bear.

"It's after midnight, and your adrenaline has been spiking repeatedly for the last hour. You're crashing. Close your eyes. I've got you."

She knew he meant it. She could feel it. Which was why, after almost being struck by lightning, crushed by a falling tree, and breaking into a cottage, Brooke felt safe enough to fall asleep in his arms.

CHAPTER 17

AARON WENT from dead asleep to wide awake when the hand slapped his face. Then the knuckles on the same hand jammed him in the ear, and the ring on the middle finger caught a lock of his hair.

Before she did any more damage, Aaron caught Brooke's hand. He gave it a gentle shake. "Brooke, are you awake?"

She mumbled something but didn't fight him when he put her hand back in her lap. He grabbed her shoulders and sat her straight on the sofa, then nudged her again. "Brooke, it's morning."

He wasn't quite lying. There was faint daylight shining through the broken window in the door. Brooke had fallen asleep almost instantly the night before. He'd stayed awake for another half hour, adding another log to the fire to keep the room warm. He was up every hour after that to do it again and had finally fallen asleep around five. He guessed it was almost seven now.

He added two things to the facts he knew about Brooke: she was a restless sleeper—she'd never stopped moving on the sofa the previous night—and she was not a morning person. That part, he didn't get. She had to be at work by seven in the morning most days. She should be used to rising with the sun. Which reminded him. "Brooke? Are you working today?"

"No. I'm trying to sleep in," she mumbled. Then one eye opened and she looked at him groggily. "Aaron?" It closed, then both eyes popped open. "Aaron?"

"Rainstorm. Fallen tree. Cabin," he reminded her.

They closed again. "Right." She heaved herself forward till her elbows were planted on her knees. She grunted like it had taken all the effort in the world for her torso to get vertical. "It looks like we made it through the night." She glanced in the fireplace. The last log had broken into pieces. Not even coals remained in the fallen ash.

"We did. The rain stopped, and the sun's coming up. I would have let you sleep a little more, but I didn't know if you were working today," he said. He was used to terrible hours and long days. He hadn't thought of what it would be like being a hotel housekeeper, having to start early to have the majority of the cleaning done by noon. It made Brooke's determination to attend night classes even more impressive.

"No, I'm off today. Which is good, because I don't know how long it will take us to get home."

"Do you want to come outside with me and check it out?" Aaron offered. He wanted to know how bad it was. It would be nice if his truck was unscathed, but it wasn't his primary concern.

"Sure, let's go."

The pine laying against the cabin was small, only about twenty feet tall. Most of the limbs were too thin and flexible to cause damage, but one had knocked the screen off a window. They circled the cottage. Aside from a lot of fallen branches, everything looked to be in reasonable shape. It helped that everything had already been put away for the winter.

The front of the property was a different story. In the light of day, the spruce that had nearly hit them last night was even bigger than Aaron had realized. It covered the entire road, blocking traffic in both directions, and filled the narrow driveway. The tip of the tree lay in the back of his truck.

"That was a closer call than I realized," Brooke said when she saw it. "Is your truck damaged?"

Aaron pushed aside a couple of branches and flinched when he saw the dent in the tailgate from the impact. "Not too badly."

She peered through the boughs. "We got lucky. If it had fallen the other way, it would have taken out the power lines. We can walk out of here if we have to."

"A hike before breakfast will stimulate our appetites, right?" he said, trying to make the best of the situation.

"That's pushing it, Gillespie."

Brooke dumped the drip-filled pot into the sink and put it away. Then she gathered the towels and afghan and stored them in the truck's cab, promising to wash and return them. He swept the glass shards from the window he broke, then cleaned the fireplace. They left the cabin inside as clean as they found it.

"Are you sure we won't get in trouble?"

"It'll be fine." In fact, Aaron had no concerns at all that the Pineys would be reasonable when he explained the situation. He would replace the window today and come back later in the week to ensure things were all cleaned up, saving them from having to make a trip from Minneapolis.

"It would be awkward for you to have to arrest yourself for breaking and entering."

"I'm pretty sure that would be a conflict of interest. I'd be happy to debate it with you on our walk back to town."

They made it two lots over before Mac Mackenzie stopped them. Her was loading a chainsaw into the back of his truck, next to a stack of orange pylons and a can of gas. His eyes went wide at the sight of the bedraggled scarecrow and waterlogged monster. "Where did you two come from?"

Aaron didn't have the energy to explain, especially before coffee. "Up the road. We need a ride back to town. Can you give us a lift?"

"Sure."

"I don't think that'll be necessary, Mac, but I appreciate the offer," Brooke said, interrupting them both.

A familiar, mud-spattered green SUV rolled to a stop, then made a careful four-point turn. The SUV idled while the passenger rolled down her window. "Hi, Mom. Hi, Sheriff Gillespie."

"Morning, Jordan," he said. "Trevor, I thought you were staying at your mother's."

"I was. Then I got your text last night." Aaron had decided to text his son at the last minute, in case his ex-wife had storm damage at her place as well. With Trevor spending the night, Aaron usually would have gone straight over to help out and make sure they were okay. The tree situation made that impossible.

Trevor continued, "Then Jordan texted me this morning and asked if I could come out and pick up you and her mom, because she doesn't have her license yet. So here we are."

Aaron hadn't realized that Trevor and Jordan were good enough friends to have exchanged numbers. He'd have to do some dad-investigating to learn if that had happened before or after he and Brooke started dating.

"You look like you need a shower," Jordan said. "To warm up," she quickly added, "not because you look bad. You might want to take off that makeup, though."

"I would love a shower and a ride, thank you," Brooke said gratefully. After she fumbled twice at the door handle, Aaron stepped in and opened the door for her. She stared at the step, then heaved herself in with a grunt.

"You're really not a morning person, are you?"

"I'm a terrific morning person after my first cup of coffee," Brooke said.

"Before that, talk to her at your peril," Jordan warned him.

"You tell him, Cookie." She sounded exhausted.

"Thanks, Trev. Let me run back to the truck. We left some stuff there when we thought we'd be walking." It only took him a minute to run back and grab the blankets and towels, but by the time he got back, Brooke was asleep in the back seat.

"Did you really spend the night in Shelley's Shack?" Trevor asked once they were underway.

"Yeah."

"Was anybody else there? Stranded like you?"

His son's voice sounded strained. Then again, Trevor was pulling onto the highway, and there was a lot of traffic for him to navigate as he crossed the road to head back to town.

"No, but that's a good point. I'll check the other

cottages when I come back for my truck. I hope anyone who was stranded did find shelter. That storm was no joke."

"I swung by the house. A tree fell into the shed."

"We can fix it. The important thing is that nobody was hurt."

Trevor looked at him when they were stopped at a red light. "How did you get in? Spare key?"

"No, I broke one of the windows in the door. I'll get cleaned up, then hit Handler Hardware and replace it. Actually, I'll call Joe Piney, let him know about that and the storm damage, and offer to take care of the downed tree too, to save them the trip to Holiday Beach."

"It would be good if they didn't have to come out," Trevor agreed. "I mean, they already closed it for the year, and you were there and didn't see anything wrong inside. I can help you with the tree. I'll be able to use the chainsaw since you'll be there." The tension left his voice as he added with a cheer, "More firewood for bonfires."

"Bonfires sound cool," Jordan added, speaking for the first time.

"Maybe we can have you over for one soon," Aaron offered.

"Okay."

He'd mentioned it to Brooke before, and she'd been agreeable. Knowing that her daughter was too—that Jordan was willing to spend some time with him and Trevor—let Aaron breathe a little easier. He wasn't thinking of creating an instant family but having both teenagers willing to let them figure things out meant a lot.

Trevor pulled into the visitor parking spot behind the Portmans' apartment. It took them a minute to wake Brooke, and another minute to get her out of the car. She kissed him absently on the cheek, thanked Trevor for the ride, then let Jordan walk her into the building.

"Wow, she is so not a morning person," Trevor said.

"That's an understatement."

"But I like her anyway.

Aaron smiled. "Me too."

CHAPTER 18

IT WASN'T a perfect evening for a bonfire. It had rained again the day before, and the clouds were still hanging around, so the chairs and logs around the Gillespie firepit weren't completely dry. The moon and stars stayed hidden, but Aaron had enough lights in the backyard and shining through the window to keep them from stumbling around in the dark.

The fire, though, was wondrous. The pit itself was a steel barrel cut in half, dropped a foot into the earth. Large, curved bricks three layers thick encircled it, giving them enough of a lip to set their feet on without risk of melting the soles of their shoes. A garden hose snaked its way between the two Adirondack chairs closest to the house.

The fire had been roaring when they arrived, the flames jumping four feet high and sparks showering twice that height when the heat ignited sap left in the wood. Now the fire had died back, and logs had settled. A bank of coals glowed red in the evening light and pumped out heat to keep the chill out of the air, but it wasn't warm enough for them to take off their jackets.

"Dad, now?" Trevor asked.

"I think it's time," he agreed.

Brooke watched the teenager sprint back into the house. "Time for what?"

"S'mores. I'm not saying my son is a chocolate addict—"

"But I am," Trevor shouted from the door.

"—but in this case, he's right. A fire isn't a fire without s'mores."

"October is the best time for s'mores because of all the mini candy bars available. It's a wonderland of chocolate goodness. They're even better on a weeknight because of an in-service day at the school. Chocolate and days off are the perfect combination," Jordan said.

"Jordan is another chocolate afficionado," Brooke offered. This was a very laid-back getting-to-know-you conversation she had no worries about.

"At least I have good taste when it comes to Halloween candy, unlike some people," her daughter teased.

"Trevor and I have an agreement. He goes trick or treating and gets all the chocolates, and I get all the gummy candies if l let him off the hook for his weekend chores," Aaron shared.

"You're a grown-up. You can buy yourself a box of Swedish berries," Brooke said.

"Making Trevor do the work is more fun."

"I heard that," Trevor said as he returned with a tray covered in graham cracker packages, mini-bars, and a bag of marshmallows. "I'll happily sort my trick-or-treat haul to get out of vacuuming. I hate vacuuming."

"Gummies are okay. My mom, on the other hand, has horrible taste in candy. You'll never guess what she likes." Jordan made a face like she was sucking a sour lemon.

"That awful taffy with the orange wrappers," Trevor suggested.

"Tootsie rolls," Aaron said with a shudder.

"Both good guesses for the worst candy, but no. Licorice. Even those gross packs with four short ropes of red licorice that are stuck together. She buys the leftovers after Halloween, and I have to watch her eat it till Christmas. So gross!"

"That is pretty gross, Brooke. I mean, licorice," Aaron teased.

"Licorice is a classic candy, and I stand by my choice."

"You'll be standing alone."

"More for me then," she said stubbornly. She'd caught flack her whole life for making Red Vines her first choice at the concession stand when she went to see a movie. Some people didn't know a good thing when it was right in front of them. "Take your chocolate and your gummy candies, and I'll keep all the licorice yumminess to myself."

"If we can keep the chocolate, do you still want a s'more?"

"Of course! I was being sarcastic. I still eat chocolate." She wasn't a huge fan of being teased, but if it gave Jordan and the guys something to bond over, she'd suffer it happily. Besides, it was hard to stay mad when dessert was on the table.

Jordan toasted her marshmallow carefully, only letting it turn the lightest shade of tan before she squished it between two crackers. Trevor, on the other hand, stuck his stick straight into the heart of the fire and let his marshmallow turn into a flaming, crusty black ball before assembling his s'more. Brooke accidentally had a couple black spots, and Aaron browned his like an old pro.

"How's school going, Jordan?" Aaron asked after they were stuffed with sugary goodness.

"Classes are fine. Mom needs to come in to talk to the principal after school tomorrow."

"Are you in trouble?"

"I'm going to be." She shrugged, and Brooke grinned. She already knew what was coming and looked forward to meeting with Principal Kelly. After three years of high school, they were on a first-name basis.

"Do you need help?"

"If you want to email the school board about why my first opinion piece of systematic gender bias in the district's dress code policy is a valid criticism, it might help. The board is meeting tonight. They're going to decide whether or not to accept the student council's invitation to come and discuss our proposed amendments."

Brooke laughed when Aaron blinked. Twice. If he wanted to get to know the Portmans, he was going to get the full picture. "What? Is this the thing you told me about, Brooke?" he asked.

"Yes," was all Brooke had time to say before her daughter took over the conversation.

"The school board's dress code is sexist, and on top of that, they enforce it more on female students than they do on male students. Then they double down when it comes to female students who are more developed than their peers. It's judgemental and insulting to both sexes."

"To both sexes?" Aaron parroted.

He looked shocked when Trevor chimed in. "Yeah, Dad. Nothing like being told as a teenaged boy you lack the self-control to stop yourself from sexually assaulting a girl in the classroom because you're overcome by lust after seeing her shoulders when guys are allowed to wear tank tops."

Jordan reached out to give him a high-five. So did Brooke.

Aaron leaned forward in his deck chair. "You said it was the first piece. What's the second piece going to be?"

"Gender bias in parking assignments. It comes out next week," Jordan said.

"I thought that was done by a draw. Isn't that the fairest way?" Aaron asked.

"Boys get seventy-five percent of the spots."

"What?" Outrage was plain on his red face. "That's not fair. Student spots should be fifty-fifty, or close enough after a draw. How has nobody noticed before?"

"Oh, the leftover parking spots are split about fifty-fifty. The problem is the football team getting first dibs on the student spots."

"That's always been a perk for the team," Trevor said.

"A perk not available to any female students." Jordan raised her eyebrows, daring them to say something.

Aaron frowned. "The boys have earned it. They've made it to State."

"The women's volleyball team has made it to State twice in the last five years. The football team has only made it once. Why doesn't the most successful team get it?"

"Because volleyball isn't football," Aaron said. Then he snapped his mouth shut. "I'm pretty sure I just put my foot in it."

"That's not fair," Trevor said.

"For you or for me?" Jordan asked. "I didn't mean to

start a fight tonight. No matter which side people are on, it's going to get everybody talking. Hence, planning on Mom spending yet more quality time with Principal Kelly and having to go to more school board meetings with me."

Her little girl once asked her if she caused too much trouble. Brooke's immediate response was, "Not at all." Brooke had done her share of fighting the good fight, and she wasn't done yet. The fact that her daughter was still protesting dress codes like her mother had twenty years earlier was infuriating.

"Speaking of the school board, how did your meeting go with them about the book, Brooke?" Aaron asked.

She was grateful for the subject change; his son didn't look impressed with Jordan at the moment. As for the meeting, Aaron had told her that he wasn't going to be able to attend that meeting, but he hadn't asked about it since. She thought he'd forgotten about it entirely. "They're considering their literature options for the second semester. Mr. Tambo was not amused. I was. Team Portman, dragging the Holiday Beach School Board into the new millennium one book at a time."

"Even though the new millennium started more than two decades ago," Jordan noted.

"We didn't live here then," Brooke quipped.

"I, for one, will welcome our new benevolent literary overlords. Anyone who can annoy Mr. Tambo and drag him out of his boring 1950s world vision is a friend of mine," Trevor said.

The kids each made themselves another s'more. Brooke begged off due to sugar overload. Aaron joked around about making Trevor run around the block to wear off his extra energy, but he was less exuberant than he'd been at the start of the evening.

When Trevor and Jordan took the leftover ingredients back into the house, Brooke dragged her chair closer to Aaron. "You got quiet."

"Do you know how many times I've been called to the principal's office for something Trevor's done?"

"He seems a pretty good kid. Twice?"

"Never. Don't you get frustrated when they call you in because of Jordan?"

Brooke got frustrated by the never-ending battle. She was weary of explaining that equal wasn't a bad word. But tired of supporting her daughter? "I would if she was called in for doing something stupid, but she's not. So, no. I'm proud of her."

"I don't think Trevor is as civic-minded as Jordan. We have very different children."

"But we both have great children, which is the important thing."

"I have to admit I'm having trouble seeing your side. I'd be mad at Trevor, but you're right there swinging away with her."

"I'm a grown-up. People can ignore kids. They have a harder time sticking their fingers in their ears and singing "la-la-la" when there's another adult in the room. Besides, somebody's got to do it."

She could tell he didn't like her answer. Thin lines spread across his forehead. His hands opened and fingers splayed, then clenched tight again. She planned to give him a minute to speak his mind before asking him outright, but he only need thirty seconds. "I'm thinking back to the protest outside City Hall this past May. The one with the news crew from Duluth. You were there," he noted.

"The town council wasn't going to repair the entrance

ramp to the library after they closed it for repairs in February, but they were prepared to double the fireworks budget for the Fourth of July display. People needed the ramp. All we did was present them with the opportunity to see how their decisions appeared to the public, especially when it affected local citizens and not just visiting tourists."

He sighed deeply. "Do you have any other protests planned besides the ones with the school board? Other wrongs to be righted? Voters' rights? Health care access? Save the whales?"

"Save the whales? In Minnesota?"

"Still, should I get you a cape for your birthday?"

"It's not for a few months, but a cape is a great idea. But no, I don't have any protests on the calendar at the moment."

"Good. I think it would really hamper our relationship if I had to arrest you."

"Only if you arrest the other guy too, because he will have it coming."

He sighed again, but this one had a bit of humor to it. "It's not going to be easy with you, is it?'"

Brooke laughed. "I thought we already discussed this. No, it's not but it'll be worth it."

CHAPTER 19

AARON PAUSED as he scraped the razor across his face. He could admit it to himself: he'd been worried after the bonfire. He knew that Brooke had a good heart but hearing about how often she and Jordan campaigned for change made him realize that it was going to be difficult if their paths crossed when he was in uniform. On the other hand, he respected her ethics and couldn't ask her not to be herself.

Fortunately, tonight was all about celebrating with no controversies involved. He was taking Brooke out for a nice dinner celebrating the fact she was done with the monstrous assignment she'd been working on that had been filling so many of her evenings. She'd been putting in tons of hours on top of her weekly class and study group.

"Whoa, Dad, hot date?"

He was in a dark navy suit, white shirt, and red tie. At Trevor's words, he stood straighter. "Celebratory supper for Brooke."

"Did she get a new job or something?"

"No, she finished a big project for school."

"That's cool. Tell her congratulations for me."

He was happy to note that Brooke was treating their night at Colombo's as a big occasion as well when he arrived to pick her up. She looked stunning in a dark blue dress with silver threads running through it. Unlike him, she had a proper jacket. Between her high heels and short skirt, it took her an extra minute to get into his truck.

She fidgeted the entire drive to the Italian restaurant. At first, he thought it was nerves, but she was smiling too hard to be worried about something. Aaron waited until the waitress had left with their order before he leaned over the table. "What's up with you?" he asked.

"I got some news."

Aaron grinned. He loved playful Brooke. "Are you going to share?"

"Maybe later."

And then she made him wait. Through the breadsticks. Through the Caesar salad. When he saw the waitress returning with their meals, he slapped his hands on the table. "Tell me! I can't take the stress anymore."

But then Brooke waited till they'd been served, and she had her napkin in her lap. Then the waitress had to refill her water glass. Brooke took a sip, staring him in the eyes the entire time. "Okay, I guess I can tell you."

"Thank you."

"As I said, I got some news." She broke off a piece of her breadstick.

"Do you remember how I said arresting you may put a damper on our relationship? It might be worth it if you don't tell me."

"Fine." Her smile was breathtaking. "Somebody got

an A on her accounting assignment, and the second-highest mark in the entire class."

"That's terrific! You must be ecstatic." She'd been working incredibly hard for that class. Aaron had never seen anyone wear the numbers off the buttons on a calculator before.

"I'm thrilled. Next is the midterm at the end of the month, so now I have to switch over to study mode, but I'll make it work. How about you? How's work?" Brooke asked.

"Same old, same old." He didn't want to tell her the truth because Brooke's good humor about her schoolwork was exactly what he needed after a long week.

As Holiday Beach moved deeper into October, the number of calls the station received had started to climb. He'd had two callouts to Jackson Farm during the week: once for a group of young men who'd snuck in a couple bottles of booze and started harassing other maze-goers, and once for a nine-year-old girl who decided it would be fun to hide from her parents and not come out even when the announcement that the maze was closing was broadcast over the loudspeakers. Over an hour later, in the dark and cold and damp, he'd found the kid cowering in a corner, crying and freaked out by the sounds of nature. Aaron was certain she was going to develop a phobia like Brooke's after that experience.

As the days drew closer to Halloween, experience said it was only going to get worse. Family Farm Grocery was going to start limiting toilet paper sales to adults next week; Handler Hardware was doing the same for spray paint. Then would come the calls from concerned citizens reporting arms hanging out of trunks, or the guy with the bullet wound walking down Main Street because the caller didn't recognize zombie makeup. Aaron liked Halloween as much as the next person, but it made his job extra challenging.

They chatted more about her course during the meal, but during dessert, the conversation took a serious turn. "I don't mind Trevor having friends over. At least I know where he is. I don't want to be rude, but having Caleb over for a sleepover almost every Friday night is starting to drag. I miss having my house to myself."

"Almost every week?"

"While Trevor's with me. Don't get me wrong, Caleb's never in the way and always polite, but he's always there. I don't remember sleepovers being this popular when Trevor was smaller." He knew his son wasn't getting into trouble, but the near-weekly events weren't something he'd done in his sophomore year.

"Maybe he's trying to get it all in before he goes away to college next year," Brooke suggested.

"Maybe. All I know is that he's going to his mother's the weekend after next, and I'll have the place all to myself. Would you like to come over for dinner two weeks from tonight?"

"I'd love to."

The conversation moved on, but part of it kept circling in his head after he dropped Brooke off for the night. Sure enough, when he got home, the familiar music of Trevor's favorite video game floated up from the basement. He staked out the kitchen, knowing the boys would resurface for snacks soon enough.

About ten minutes later, the music paused, and he heard footsteps on the stairs. Trevor arrived in the kitchen with a handful of soda cans which he threw into the recycling bin and an empty nacho bag. Aaron expected Caleb to appear but then heard the sounds of the shower from the downstairs bathroom.

"Hey, kid, got a minute?" he asked.

"Sure, Dad."

"Is Caleb taking a shower?"

"Yeah."

This was a fine line. "I've noticed his been over a lot since school started."

Trevor's response was slower this time. "Yeah. Is that okay?"

"It is. You weren't such good friends last year."

"No. We started hanging out this summer. He's been working with me on Mac's property. We had a lot of the same classes last year too."

"Do his folks mind him spending so much time over here?" Aaron pressed gently. Despite his best efforts, he hadn't been able to track down the Quentins for Lucy. While Caleb said hi when he arrived at the house, Trevor tended to rush them to the basement as soon as they arrived. Aaron knew he'd have a problem if Trevor spent more time out of the house than at home. Teenagers were supposed to push their limits, but they still had them.

His son's shoulders crept towards his ears. "Not really." Aaron recognized the look, so he waited patiently. "He has some problems at home. His parents aren't great."

"Is this something you need an adult for?"

"Not yet?" Trevor didn't sound sure. "It's handled for now, but if it gets worse, I might need to talk to you. But not yet."

"Just don't forget I'm here, Trevor. So's your mother. So is Brooke. We can help."

"We know. Thanks."

The shower downstairs stopped.

"Lights out by midnight, even if it is a Friday night. I don't need Zombie Trev tomorrow. We have to start prepping the yard for winter. First is organizing your gigantic wood pile into stacks so it doesn't look like our backyard was hit by a tornado."

"You've got it, Dad."

That conversation hadn't gone as well as he'd hoped. He was certain there was a reason Caleb had practically moved in on Fridays. "Not great parents" left a lot of options open. The kid was safe and fed while he was here. Aaron hadn't seen any bruises. All he could do was let the boys know his door was open.

CHAPTER 20

BROOKE WOKE to a gorgeous sunrise in an empty apartment—but couldn't stay in bed and enjoy it. She was working the Saturday morning shift at the Dew Drop Inn, and a bachelorette party were checking out, so there would be several rooms to clean. She'd hoped to talk to Jordan before she left, but her daughter had to work even earlier than she did. She was pleased that Jordan was trusted to open the store, but it was time to check in to see if Jordan's part-time paid job was interfering with her full-time student job when she saw her later today.

When she arrived at work, Brooke was surprised to see Mickey Wagner standing behind the reception desk handing the check-outs, and Lucy Callahan coming down the stairs with a toolbox in her hand and a garbage bag held at arm's length in the other. Lucy saw her, shook her head, and walked down the hall.

The lobby, which had been painted a fresh cream in the spring, appeared to be in one piece. The marble inlay at the entrance and the floors appeared reasonably clean, but Brooke planned to mop them anyway. The looks she was getting from the hotel's staff encouraged her to find something else to do first.

"We've taken a cursory look at your rooms and have documented what we found. The Dew Drop Inn will be putting a significant damage charge onto your credit cards. If we find additional damage, there will be more fees. Also, the goat has been returned to Jackson Farms. Any costs resulting from that will be between you and the farm and will be completely separate from these charges."

The woman at the desk had clothes and an ombré dye job that screamed she was from the city. Her thick makeup did nothing to hide the dark circles under her eyes or her fat lip. "This is ridiculous. I'm the bride-to-be. I'm not paying a damage deposit. It was an accident. Let me speak to the manager. He's a personal friend of the family."

"You didn't *accidentally* bring a goat that you stole from a corn maze into your suite. You didn't *accidentally* feed it all the ingredients from the honor bar, because the wrappers and empty cans were in the garbage. And I can guarantee you, ma'am, that the manager is not going to give you a pass, because *I* am the owner of this hotel."

Sometimes it was nice to see comeuppance being delivered in person, Brooke thought. Especially when it sounded like she'd be cleaning up after a goat. She was not counting on a tip from those guests.

The woman stomped away in black-soled, high-heeled boots that left scuffs on the tile floor. Mickey waited till she joined the group of women huddled by the meeting room, then waved her over. He ran his hand through his short brown hair, then offered her a rueful smile. "It's bad," he said in greeting. "I called in Lucy because we're going to need repairs after the mess is cleaned up. You'll be getting hazard pay today."

Brooke didn't mind the fact that she worked hard for her money. She did resent it when people went out of their way to make her work harder. "Do you want me to do all the other rooms and leave it till last, or tackle it first?"

"Get the other rooms in order first. I have no idea how long that one will take," Mickey said.

It took her two and a half hours, and that was with Lucy's help.

"A goat? Really?" Lucy grumbled as they manhandled a king-size mattress down the staircase into the lobby, then dragged it to the dumpster behind the building. "Some people have more money than sense. It's a shame it didn't go after their three-hundred-dollar shoes instead of the furniture."

"I'm going to record every spot of dirt and damage so Mickey can bill them to the cent for this mess," Brooke said when she returned to the room. In addition to the destroyed bed and linens, they also had to take down and replace the curtains and remove a dresser that had two knobs and a corner chewed off.

Then Brooke was able to start cleaning.

She'd been right. The occupants hadn't left a tip. However, her very generous and guilt-ridden boss had given her the promised bonus, which meant she was absolutely not cooking dinner after the disgusting day she'd had. Images of dancing burgers, burritos, and pizza all vied for her attention.

She arrived at home with a large order of loaded nachos, telling herself that the chopped tomatoes and onions and olives almost made it a salad.

Jordan followed her nose into the kitchen. "Do I smell"—she sniffed the air—"nachos? Restaurant nachos?"

"I got a disaster bonus."

Her daughter frowned. "How bad?"

"About an eleven."

Jordan's nose crinkled. "People can be so gross."

"It's incentive to keep studying, that's for sure," Brooke agreed.

Once the meal was plated and they were fighting over the sour cream, Brooke realized how much she didn't want to have the conversation about work that she needed to. Before she started, her phone buzzed with a text from Aaron. "Must cancel Sunday morning coffee. Break-in paperwork and meetings." His news capped off an already terrible day.

"What's with the sigh?" Jordan asked.

"I was supposed to have coffee with Aaron tomorrow since I was working today, but he had to cancel. He's dealing with a break-in."

"Where? I hope nobody was hurt."

"*Where?*" she texted Aaron.

"*Austen Cottage.*"

Jordan's jaw dropped at the news. "That makes me glad I wasn't at any of the Halloween parties last night."

She'd never suspect Jordan of vandalism, but knowing her daughter had been at work was an extra comfort. "You and me both, Cookie."

"Are there any suspects?"

Brooke waved her phone. "You know what I know. I don't know how much Aaron can tell us, but I'm sure the rumor mill will have all the news by morning. Are you working tomorrow?"

"I have an afternoon shift."

"Then you'll hear all about it."

"Speaking of gossip, what did I hear about you and a goat?" Jordan asked.

The nachos were long gone by the time Brooke finished recounting her day. Halfway through her story, Jordan got up and returned with a bottle of iced tea from Brooke's secret stash.

"I think I'll let you have the living room and remote to yourself tonight," Jordan said. "You deserve a little downtime. No studying! Give yourself the night off."

"We're not done yet, Cookie. There's something else we need to discuss."

Jordan slumped in her favorite corner of the sofa and pulled a pillow into her lap, putting a barrier between them. Brooke recognized that move. "What?"

"That attitude is not going to make this go any easier. When you started working, we made an agreement that it was dependent on maintaining your grades and other things. This is your check-in. If you aren't mature enough to have this conversation, I question if you're ready for an adult job."

"Okay. What would you like to talk about?"

The attitude was still there, hidden under a layer of bitingly polite sarcasm. It wasn't outright rude, but Jordan was tapdancing on the line. "How are your classes? Are you giving yourself enough time for studying and your homework? How are your teachers? Any problems? What's the news with volleyball? And the drama club? Are you getting any pushback from your school board stories?" She didn't fire them out like the questions were coming from a machine gun. She laid them on the table and let Jordan decide which ones she was going to answer. "If I hear the word 'fine,' we are going to have a much more unpleasant discussion."

"I have two heavy classes this semester. Senior math and chemistry are going okay. I'm giving them a majority of my study time," her daughter began.

It took a lot of prodding and leading questions, but Brooke eventually got an update on Jordan's history and gym classes as well. Jordan also gave her the news that the school had announced a new book for the next semester's English class. It wasn't one of Brooke's top choices, but it represented life in the last thirty years rather than sixty, so it was an improvement.

"Nobody wants to replace Mrs. Bellingham, so unless she comes back for the second semester, the drama club is done. Which sucks because I wanted to do one more play before I graduated, but there aren't enough teachers."

Brooke nodded in understanding. That was the problem with small-town schools. There were fewer teachers and only so much extra time to go around. "How has the response been to your stories?" she asked.

"The students are for changes to the dress code. The school board accepted the student council's invitation to discuss the issue on Wednesday."

"And the parking spot article?"

"That comes out on Wednesday too." Jordan hesitated. "Trevor's dad was not impressed with that."

"Nobody likes to be confronted with the fact they're benefiting at the expense of others. It doesn't mean they're right."

"Is it going to cause problems between the two of you? Trevor's on the football team."

"Oh, Cookie, not at all." Brooke moved the pillow and

sat beside Jordan, pulling her into a hug. "Don't ever worry about that. Aaron is a grown man. He's not going to get mad at anyone for having different opinions than he does. Besides, he already admitted that the parking situation isn't fair. He has to come to terms with it. I wouldn't go out with somebody who didn't recognize right from wrong." She hoped Jordan could feel her conviction. She believed in Aaron, truly believed he was a good man. She wasn't blindly calling him perfect, but what she'd seen and heard gave her the confidence to trust him to come around to the right side.

"I guess you really like him, huh?"

"I really do."

"He seems nice, and he's nice to you. I guess I can like him too."

CHAPTER 21

AARON WATCHED the glass tray in the microwave spin as it warmed his leftover pizza. The rubbery cheese and dried-out crust would be the nicest meal he'd had in days. He was bone-tired, totally flummoxed and dangerously cranky. He was grateful that Trevor was at football practice because he was in no shape for human company.

He was dead on his feet. He was used to being called out to deal with all kinds of hijinks, but this week had pushed his patience with Halloween pranks to the limit. Sightings of people hiding and running through the back woods of Shakespeare Drive had him tromping through the bush at all hours. It wasn't just Neil Dempsey calling the station with tales of spooky figures trespassing in the night. Even level-headed Mac had reported figures lurking around his building site and breaking into his storage trailer.

He ate his pizza, washed off the tomato sauce that had dripped onto his chin, popped a beer, and settled onto the couch with his tablet in front of him to call Brooke.

She answered right away. The wall behind her sofa

had little jack-o'-lantern lights hanging from a string, and he spied a plastic pail of candy in the corner of the screen.

"Hey there, sheriff. Catch any bad guys today?"

Aaron held his thumb and forefinger an inch apart. "Missed them by this much."

"I'm sorry to hear that. Justice will have to wait for another day. Can you talk about what happened?" she asked.

"Sean Fitzpatrick got very lucky," Aaron said. "Mac swung by his property because there's been a lot of cars parked on Shakespeare Drive lately in the evenings that he didn't recognize. He thought he saw somebody sneaking out of Shelley's Shack and called me. They were gone when I got there, but I checked the neighboring properties. I spotted an unfamiliar navy, extended cab pickup at Austen Cottage. They kicked in the front door and headed right for the liquor cabinet."

"That's horrible. Who was it?"

"That I can't comment on."

"Do you think that will calm things down now?" Brooke asked.

"I really hope so. We have two and a half more weeks till Halloween. I'm going to burn out by then if this keeps up." Aaron wasn't kidding in the slightest. He hadn't had a solid night's sleep in weeks, even when he was home. He was going through antacids like candy, and he couldn't see an end in sight, even after Halloween.

"I know you aren't a big police department, but can't any of your deputies take any of these callouts? It can't all fall on your shoulders. You're only one man," Brooke said, her voice full of sympathy. "A really handsome, smart, funny man, but you are one of a kind."

He snorted. It wasn't much of a laugh, but it loosened

some of the tension in his gut. "I don't want to give them all the bad shifts."

"How about giving them a percentage so you aren't stuck with ninety-nine percent? You need a break, Aaron. Not only for your mental health, but for your physical health. I'm worried about you."

He almost brushed her concern off. Almost. Until she added that last comment. He knew he'd been pushing too hard for too long. Summers were long in Holiday Beach. Tripling the population tripled the problems. He'd forgotten to come out of high law enforcement mode. "Thanks, Brooke. I appreciate it. But I'm fine."

"I'm serious, Aaron. When's the last time you took a vacation?"

He shrugged.

"Everybody needs downtime. Maybe we could take a day after my midterm. Go into Minneapolis for the day or something, just the two of us."

"I'll look at the schedule tomorrow."

"In the meantime, eat a vegetable, have a glass of milk, and go to bed. You look beat," Brooke said. "Sleep well, Sheriff Tall, Funny, and Handsome."

"Sleep well yourself, Numbers Lady."

Aaron was actually able to do as he was told. He wasn't on call that night, but he was the two following evenings. When he set the next week's roster, he was going to give himself more time off. He'd been trying to make things easy for his deputies for the last couple months, knowing they were all pulling extra hours, but it was time to even out the schedule.

He didn't eat a vegetable, but he did have a glass of milk before he went to bed. For the first time in ages, he slept all the way through. And dreamed of Brooke.

CHAPTER 22

BROOKE PORTMAN DID NOT ENJOY BEING SUMMONED to the high school. She'd been asked to see the principal more than once, but she'd never been ordered to appear under a threat to her daughter's future.

Brooke arrived at the high school ten minutes later than she'd intended, but some things were more important. Taking the time to dress to the nines, in her only good suit and heels and with her hair in a no-nonsense chignon, was worth the delay. Because she meant business and she wanted everybody who saw her to know it.

If they wanted to play hardball, she was going to bring the bat.

Jordan's article on the bias in the student parking spot assignments had gone live on the website that morning. She'd had over thirty hits before she'd left for school that morning. She'd added a hundred more by the time Brooke had left their apartment. John Reno, the faculty advisor for the paper, had wisely turned off comments, insisting that any responses be emailed to the school with the sender's contact information attached.

They'd discussed it before: John, Brooke, and Jordan. They'd expected a reaction. What Brooke hadn't realized was that today was the day the school board was visiting to discuss the dress code with the student council. From the sounds the office secretary made when she called, the board members were not pleased with Jordan's latest piece. One in particular demanded Jordan post a retraction immediately.

By all reports, things had gone downhill after that.

The high school was a madhouse. The walls were papered with posters about the upcoming football games and signs for the Halloween dance at the end of the month. Several notices advising students that costumes were only acceptable on Halloween itself or at the dance. That didn't stop some of them from decorating their lockers.

The adults on the scene were the ones doing the yelling. The students forming a wall between the over-dressed woman and the door to the newspaper room were red-faced but holding their tempers for now. Principal Kelly stood on the sidelines like a referee nobody was listening to. John Reno was blocking the entrance to the room.

Brooke showed no fear. She strode through the narrow gap until the adults were forced to step back and give way. "Excuse me, Principal Kelly, I was summoned?" If she could have left frost in the air with her words, she would have.

"Your daughter owes the school board an apology after her false accusations," a woman said.

"I don't think we've been officially introduced. You are?" There was a reason Brooke had worn her power suit. She knew exactly who she'd be dealing with.

Marjory Major was the board member who'd declined to be introduced to her when she'd made her presentation regarding the board's literature choices. She'd also refused to address Brooke directly afterward. Everybody in the corridor knew it.

"I'm Marjory Major."

"This situation sounds serious. Please tell me, in detail and for the videos being recorded by these various students, what false accusations has my daughter made against the school board? I read the articles she's published, as has Mr. Reno, the newspaper's faculty advisor. Everything Jordan said was factual, and documentation was provided by the school and from the school board's own public policies and minutes."

"I am not a sexist!"

"Good for you. But Jordan didn't call you a sexist. She said the existing policies, which the current board didn't make, were sexist. But that distinction doesn't answer my question. What false accusations has she made?" Brooke repeated. "It's true that the football players are issued spots before the rest of the student body has a chance to enter the draw. Principal Kelly confirmed that it's school policy. Basic math says that fifty players and a hundred spots means that the football team gets half. The school, board, and state all confirm that the girls' volleyball team has made it to state finals twice in the last five years, and the football team has only made it to the playoffs once, so the volleyball team is the 'winningest' team in the school. If the policy is to give the spots to the team with the best record, they should go to the volleyball team."

"That's not how things are done," Marjory yelled in her face, spittle flying.

Brooke drew a tissue from her pocket and dabbed her

cheek. "Jordan didn't say that wasn't how things are done. She said the policy was sexist and biased towards the football team, which is all male. She asked if the board had any intention of changing them to provide equality to all students when it came to parking space allotments."

Brooke faced Marjory head-on. "So, I ask you again, what is the problem here, and why was I ordered to the school? As far as I can see, my daughter has done nothing wrong. You, on the other hand, are literally spitting mad and are hurling verbal abuse at a minor. Several minors," she amended, catching a glimpse of Olivia Holiday, the student newspaper editor, her face pale but determined.

"Every last student involved with this post will be expelled unless they retract all the columns that disparage the school board," Marjory threatened. "The board will also deal with the faculty advisor."

"We both know you can't expel anyone for this, Ms. Major," Brooke said. She'd had a long discussion with Principal Kelly about repercussions for Jordan's op-ed pieces. Expulsion wasn't one of them.

"I can shut down the website," Marjory countered

"That you can do," Brooke agreed.

Marjory gave her a vicious smirk.

"But there's nothing to keep them from reposting it elsewhere. Again, the truth is the truth. Free speech and all that. These delightful, civic-minded, equality-demanding young people can only present their case. The board's decision and how they choose to present it to the community is the board's business."

Brooke hadn't drawn a line in the sand, she had carved it into a concrete pad. She knew from years of experience and a lot of advice that the surest way to lose a confrontation was to get emotional. It gave the opponent an edge. Cold facts trumped all. If she didn't fold to the social pressure of dealing with a board member who was prominent in the community—and years of being "only a housekeeper" had accustomed her to that pressure—Marjory's options were to throw a public fit, which would weaken her case, or save face, walk away, and try to find another way to get what she wanted.

Unfortunately for Marjory, she went with the first option.

Brooke, at five-foot-four, was not a tall woman, even in heels. Marjory Major towered over her and gave the impression she did it a lot to get her way. Then she got even louder. "This is unacceptable! If she were my daughter, she'd learn some respect. If you won't teach it to her, I will."

"There is nothing you can teach that a decent human being needs to learn."

Marjory raised her hand to her shoulder as if to strike, but Brooke caught her wrist before she could.

"Assault! You saw her assault me, Principal Kelly! I'm pressing charges."

Brooke released her arm and took half a step back. Then she sighed. The board member ranted to the principal, naming every person in the school she felt had insulted her, not treated her with the respect befitting her position, or not jumped on demand. Her arms flailed as she pointed out people. For a second time, her hand came too close to Brooke's face for comfort, so Brooke grabbed it, held it for a second, and then threw it down.

"Ms. Portman, I need you to stop touching Ms. Major."

"Ms. Major has almost hit me in the face twice in the last two minutes. The videos will confirm this. I will not let her assault me because she's throwing a temper tantrum. If she wishes to continue her violent physical behavior, she should ensure she isn't within striking distance of innocent bystanders." Brooke wasn't rude. She didn't shout, she didn't accuse, even though she wanted to, wanted to so badly she thought her head would explode from the pressure and anger inside her skull—but she held her temper.

"She has a point, Ms. Major," Principal Kelly agreed. His face looked extra red against his blond beard.

"I will calm down but, at the very least, an apology is in order. A public apology. There have been some grievous public insults issued today," Marjory insisted.

Principal Kelly looked at her but addressed Marjory. "An apology doesn't sound unreasonable."

"I can live with that," Brooke said. She knew what she was about to do would demolish the entire "give a little, get along" philosophy the other adults had going. She also knew she wasn't in the wrong in doing it. "Ms. Major can apologize to me and Jordan at any time."

"You're delusional. I'm not apologizing to either of you. You, however, can apologize to me, and if it's good enough, I'll consider not pressing charges." Marjory crossed her arms. For a moment, Brooke had a flash of what the woman would have looked like as a stubborn four-year-old. This, however, was forty years later.

"So much for that plan."

"Please, ladies, don't get emotional," Principal Kelly pleaded.

Something inside her cracked. "Excuse me? I'm too emotional?" Brooke repeated. She concentrated on keeping her voice completely flat. "Why would you say that? I've been perfectly calm through this entire situation. I didn't scream at anybody. I didn't almost hit people in the face. I didn't threaten to expel students. I am not the one who needs to calm down. I have been, and continue to be, nothing but calm. I have done nothing that requires an apology, and neither has my daughter."

"Ms. Portman, you grabbed her."

"Principal Kelly, are you saying a woman has to let a hand make contact with her face before she's allowed to defend herself from an assault?"

"No, I'm not saying that," he responded quickly.

"I didn't think so." She shifted her attention. "Ms. Major, I'm not doing anything wrong. Neither has Jordan or anybody else on the newspaper staff. This situation is entirely of your own making. How you handle it is your decision. As are the consequences. Just like I have my own decisions and consequences to deal with. This isn't me being difficult. This is life."

"We'll see about that. And we'll see about those assault charges." Then Marjory walked away with her head held high, silk scarf flapping behind her, like she hadn't lost the battle. The rest of the war lay ahead.

Mr. Reno stepped up. "Here's what's happening. I'm requesting that anybody who filmed or is still filming this encounter to please email me a copy of their video or a link to it. If you are a student who doesn't have any reason to be in the corridor after school hours, I'm going to ask that you leave for the day."

The principal stepped forward. "Everybody not involved with the newspaper is dismissed. Ms. Jacobs, our school counsellor, is still in her office and is in tomorrow if you want to discuss what happened here." The red-faced man waited a moment. "Dismissed means you need to go. *Now.*"

A dozen students slowly moved toward the door.

"Next," Principal Kelly continued, "if you are involved with the newspaper, you are free to go do whatever it is you should be doing as long as you do it somewhere other than the hall. That includes you, Jordan, unless you want to go home with your mother."

"I'll wait for my mom in the newspaper room."

Brooke hated that her daughter sounded so uncertain. "I'll knock when it's time to go, Cookie."

The rest of the students dispersed. Mr. Reno followed them into the newspaper room and closed the door behind him.

"That could have gone better," Principal Kelly said. "It could have gone a lot worse, but it was bad timing the story came out on the same day the board was visiting the school to discuss the dress code with the student council. I want to reiterate that we are standing behind Jordan on these stories. Only staff are looking at the emails her pieces have generated. There's been a lot of pushback."

"I'm sure. She's convinced it will make a good college essay."

"We've weeded out the commenters who don't have children in the school. Most still think the current parking assignment policy should stay, but it's not an overwhelming majority."

Brooke longed to pull her sweat-soaked blouse away from her back now that her adrenaline rush was fading. But something held her back, something that said it wasn't entirely safe to drop her guard yet, even if it was down to the two of them. "It's hard to give up a perk, especially when it's a tradition. Jordan isn't the first person to bring this up. She's just the first to do it in a time when people are more willing to listen."

"Unfortunately, Marjory is not one of those people."

"Do you think she'll actually press charges?" she asked.

"I wouldn't be surprised if she did. She'd at least look into it to be a nuisance."

Knowing what she did about Marjory, Brooke wasn't surprised at this observation. She let herself have a minute. She'd solved one problem—Marjory coming after Jordan—but had created another. Marjory's real problem wasn't Jordan; it was the board's policy. That was something for her and the board to sort out. Brooke would go to the meeting and state her opinion, but she didn't have to do the work to provide the solution. That was their job.

The door to the newspaper room cracked open. "It is safe to come out?" Jordan asked.

"It's fine." Brooke took a breath. She had to refocus. "How are you?"

"That was bad," Jordan said.

She looped her arm around her daughter's shoulders and said goodbye to Principal Kelly and Mr. Reno. They headed for the parking lot. "You know I'll be watching the videos. Is there anything you want to tell me first?"

"No. Three members of the school board met with the student council. That didn't go well either, but Olivia is the president of the student council and president of the debate club, so she kept the meeting on track and only discussed the dress code. It wasn't much of an argument when she pulled out the actual code and read it aloud. Then Ms. Major came by the newspaper office. Principal Kelly was right on her heels, and he and Mr. Reno kept it under control until you got here."

Her brave, beautiful daughter paused. "Ms. Major said she was going to press charges. I can apologize—"

"Oh, no," Brooke protested. "Out of everything that happened this afternoon, that in particular had nothing to do with you. Marjory was talking out of her butt trying to save face. It was an intimidation tactic and nothing more. You are always allowed to defend yourself if a fist is coming near your face. I'm not apologizing for that."

"What if she does talk to the sheriff? I started this whole thing..."

"Again, Cookie, not your problem. I promise."

"Okay."

Jordan stared out the window. She was saying all the right things, so Brooke let it go for now. Her daughter didn't have the life experience yet on how to handle the pressure that was leftover. Brooke would check on her again later that evening to see how she was handling the second wave of emotions.

"Thanks for coming so fast."

"Of course. But I don't feel like cooking after that. What do you say to frozen pizza and a sleeve of Oreos for dessert?" It was comfort food at its finest.

"Iced tea with lemon?"

Her secret stash was getting a workout. "You bet. The best of everything for my best girl."

CHAPTER 23

AARON CAME HOME from the station and changed into a Henley, heavy jeans, and steel-toed work boots. Then he went into the backyard and murdered a log with his axe. He'd wasn't fit for human company until he'd worked out some of his frustrations.

First, he spent the morning dealing with the general irritation of dealing with all the paperwork from the Austen Cottage break-in. Now that Shakespeare Drive had developed a party reputation, it would be hard to lose it. He'd already updated his deputies that they'd be doing more drive-bys, trying to stomp out the rumor and party opportunities before they took a firm hold. The last thing he wanted was to get complaints from the local cabin owners; he didn't have the patience to deal with Neil Dempsey on a regular basis.

Then he'd spent the last hour of his day dealing with Marjory Major. That was time he'd never get back. She tried to get him to press assault charges against Brooke. It was a point of pride that Aaron didn't brush off official complaints. He investigated, because it was his job. In this case, it wasn't she said/she said. It was Marjory said/the video showed. Because he'd received no less than three links to the video, as well as a copy that Trevor had taken in the hallway.

He'd tried polite. He soon switched to blunt. "Ms. Major, I've seen the videos that various students took of the scene in the hall. If you insist on pressing charges, I will take notes as I watch it and save a copy as evidence. However, if I see it is self-defense as Ms. Portman claimed on the video, that means she was defending herself from your assault, and she can press charges against you. Do you still wish for me to proceed?"

Marjory opened and closed her mouth twice. Aaron saw the dilemma, plain on her face. They both knew what was on the video. Marjorie Major would deny any story the students told, but the video told the unbiased truth. Her reputation was based on the premise that everybody saw her as a paragon of virtue and equality in her role as the senior female member of the school board. She couldn't afford the truth.

"No," she finally said.

"Gender bias is a very polarizing subject. I'm sure the board will have a vigorous debate about it before bringing it to a vote, and that's not including all the input you'll be getting from parents on both sides of the parking issue. Responsibilities and issues like this are part of being on the school board. It requires a thick skin at the best of times."

"I don't like what Jordan Portman said about me."

"As Brooke Portman pointed out, her daughter wasn't talking about you. She was talking about the policy. If you feel the policy reflects badly on the board, you are lucky to be in a position to do something about it. But that is not something Jordan Portman or the Holiday Beach Police Department can fix."

She'd huffed and puffed a little more, then stormed away. Aaron felt dirty for even pretending to feel sympathy for her. His job was hard enough. When he got to do some good, when he helped somebody, when he caught a bad guy, the high was incredible; all the work was worth it. Then there were the days when he was treated like a glorified attack dog, and he wondered if it was worth it to come back to the station the next morning.

Today was an attack-dog day.

All he wanted to do was call Brooke, but since she was the one who he'd been asked to attack, he didn't know if his call would even be welcome. She hadn't had a pleasant day either.

The urge to see her face won. If she wasn't in the mood to talk, she'd let him know. He rolled the water bottle between his hands as he waited for Brooke to answer his video call. When she did, he saw that she was in her bedroom. She was sitting on her bed, with her pillows piled high against a fabric headboard. She wasn't wearing makeup or a hair band. Instead, her hair was down and tucked behind her ears, and he saw dark rings under her eyes.

"I had a frustrating afternoon with Marjory Major. How was your day?" he said.

Her eyes went wide, and she plastered an obviously fake smile on her face. "Me too! I'll bet my day was as bad as yours."

"Are you and Jordan alright? Any further problems from Marjory?" He doubted it. He'd bet that Marjory went home to lick her wounds and plot her next move with the board. Coming after a teenager had already backfired spectacularly. Aaron wouldn't want to be the paper's faculty advisor or Principal Kelly, though.

"We're okay, thank you. Like I told Jordan, dealing with Marjory is too much like *Macbeth* to worry about. The rest of the board is, if not more reasonable, less volatile."

"She's like *Macbeth*?"

Brooke blew a raspberry, making him laugh. "You know. A tale told by an idiot, full of sound and fury, signifying nothing."

"I wouldn't say that to her face."

On the screen, Brooke shrugged. "I might. At a later date. This afternoon, I wasn't going to escalate any more than I had to. It was all I could do not to snap at her smug face."

Aaron sighed and let his head hit the cushion on the sofa back. "Trevor was not impressed with the suggestion that he should lose the parking spot he got by being on the football team. We had another loud discussion about rights versus privileges. I didn't have much solid ground to stand on since I'd congratulated him when he got it, saying he'd earned it." His son had made a good point when he said it was a lot easier to suggest others make a sacrifice than it was to be the person making one.

"It's hard to admit you've changed your mind without feeling weak."

"He thinks it should be phased in so new players don't automatically get it."

"It's still not fair, but it's a compromise that will only take three years to even out. After how many decades of status quo, that is a relatively fast change. It may not be fast enough for the other students, though."

"I'm so glad he's a senior this year."

"Me too. Of course, in my case, it means whatever college Jordan goes to is going to get three or four years of policy critique."

"I win."

"There you go." She smiled, but stress lines still radiated from her eyes. "At some point, I'm going to have to speak to the school board again," she said quietly.

"Yes, but you can do it."

"I know, but I hate..."

Her voice trailed off. Aaron was surprised. She seemed fine with Jordan's newspaper op-eds. She was already ready to stand up for the underdog in any situation. Did she actually resent the confrontations where she had to fight for the right thing? It had to be exhausting. Was she just doing it for her daughter? "Hate what?"

"Formal public speaking. I can talk to people with no problem, but having to address a group? With notes? One of these days I'm going to snap, and start running round, shaking people, yelling 'Do as I say!' We'd all be so much better off if everybody listened to my genius." She sighed. "But apparently that's frowned upon. Even when I'm right."

He laughed. He couldn't help it. "I'd appreciate it if you held off on snapping at the school board till our kids have graduated." He leaned closer to the screen. "I'm not going to have to arrest you for beating Marjory with a piece of limp spaghetti someday, am I?"

"I'll promise to try to do it when you aren't on duty."

"You're all heart, Brooke."

"For you, I am. How are you doing after this afternoon?"

"I'm exhausted. I came home and chopped a cord of wood to work out my aggravation."

"How much is a cord?"

Aaron shrugged. "If I have to deal with Marjory again, I'll be good for firewood until the end of the decade."

"Poor baby," she teased.

"How goes your studying for your midterm?" Aaron asked. As soon as it was over, Brooke would have two whole weeks without an assignment or a test, and he intended to make the most of that time with her.

"It's going. It's a lot of work, though. I want to stay on the Dean's List because it will help when it comes to job placements during the internship phase so I can't let up, but I'll be glad when the midterm is done."

"We'll celebrate when you've aced it."

Her smile at his suggestion made his entire rotten day worthwhile. "I'm looking forward to it already."

CHAPTER 24

THE ONLY THING that could possibly make homework even more fun was adding trips to the laundry room in the basement between questions. Was there anything better than carrying baskets of dirty clothes down two flights of stairs to a creepy basement?

"I should have called tails," Brooke muttered to herself. Heads had to do the laundry, tails had to fold it and put it on the appropriate bed or linen shelves. Jordan had lucked out on the folding for the last three weeks. Brooke got the stairclimbing workout.

The basement wasn't *that* horrible. It didn't have damp concrete walls with a single, psycho-attracting, dim bulb swinging from a wire in the ceiling. The well-lit corridor was a butterscotch orange, which wasn't pleasant, but it was clean and fresh, thanks to Lucy putting on a new coat of paint from one of the surplus cans in the storage room. The laundry room had one cinderblock wall behind the three washers and dryers, but the others were drywalled and painted.

On the other side of the central cinderblock wall were

the building's utility rooms and a workroom for the property maintenance manager. Brooke hadn't seen inside that room.

The storage rooms along the other three outside walls weren't as nice. Their doors opened to the main corridor that ran in a U around the building. The plywood walls didn't reach the ceiling, and the fluorescent lighting ran from one locker to the next. The units were only big enough for a couple bikes or a Christmas tree and a couple boxes, but Brooke was grateful for the extra space.

After she swapped out her clothes for a basket of clean towels, Brooke could have sworn she saw a shadow pass under the door of unit one-oh-two. "Hello?" she called.

When there was no reply, she decided it had to be her imagination. There was nobody living in the associated apartment. She wasn't going to think about mice or other creatures scrabbling about in the building.

She hefted the basket with the jug of fabric softener nestled in the warm fluffy towels, then marched back up the stairs, determined to make it through the next section of her textbook before the buzzer on the stove told her it was time to switch the wash again.

Brooke kept her eyes open when she carried down the next load, a laundry hamper overflowing with T-shirts, jeans, and twice as many socks as a normal person would need in a week. She also chose her steps more carefully, placing her feet on the steps rather than stomping down them like an elephant.

There was definitely movement behind the storage unit door. A shadow blocked the light twice as she passed by. The washer thumped and rumbled on its final load for the night, so Brooke left her clothes and basket sitting on the dryer and silently reentered the corridor. As she approached storage unit one-oh-two, she heard a distinct scuff of a shoe sole hitting loose gravel on the concrete floor.

She reached out. When her fingertips hit the doorknob, she turned it slowly. Each of the lockers had a handle that only locked from the outside. If it was locked, there was vermin. If it was open, she had much bigger problems.

The knob turned for a quarter rotation before jerking to a stop. It was too far to be locked, and not enough to open the door. Someone was holding it from the inside. She twisted a little further and met resistance.

When she heard a muffled curse, she didn't stop for her laundry. She didn't slow down when she lost her slipper on the first-floor landing.

Brooke burst in her apartment and locked the door behind her. "Jordan, stay in the apartment!"

Her daughter came out of her bedroom, her silk scarf wrapped around her hair. "I wasn't planning on going anywhere, but can I ask why?"

"Somebody's in the storage units."

"O-kaaaay." She drew out the single word until it was a question.

"Someone is in the unit for one-oh-two, and it's supposed to be empty."

"Please tell me you didn't go in there like some kind of horror monster bait. You know better than that, don't you?" Jordan begged.

"I called out, but nobody answered. I didn't go in," Brooke hedged. She'd tried to but she was unsuccessful. Jordan was right; she should have known better.

"Are you going to call Lucy?"

"I'm going to call Aaron and ask him to check it out. With all the break-ins around town lately, I don't think we should confront whoever's down there on our own." Brooke dialed and put her phone on the kitchen counter.

She had one sneaker on when he picked up. "Hi, Brooke. I didn't expect to hear from you until later." His voice sounded warm and relaxed. She hated to be the person to ruin his mellow mood.

"This is an official call," she said bluntly.

"Are you in trouble?"

"I think someone has broken into a storage unit downstairs. I'm going to call Lucy to see if she's allowed somebody in there, but if she hasn't, I was hoping you could come over."

"How about I come over anyway? Just to be safe." She heard movement on the other end of the line and pictured him pulling on his jacket and boots.

"I'd appreciate it."

"Stay in your apartment."

"The door is locked, and Jordan is here with me."

"Don't go back downstairs. Don't try to keep an eye on the staircase. Don't do *anything*," Aaron emphasized. "I'll be there in fifteen minutes."

"I promise."

It was hard, though. As soon as she hung up, Brooke's internal voice began berating her for calling Aaron over something so silly. A person broke into a storage unit that she knew was empty. That wasn't an emergency. They obviously weren't stealing.

She groaned. What if it was Lucy? What if her friend was sweeping it out for the next tenant and had her earbuds in and was leaning on the door when she tried to open it? That was a much more likely scenario. She was going to scare Lucy to death.

Brooke had to warn her.

Jordan darted in front of the door. "No way, Mom. You're not going out there."

"It was probably Lucy."

"Then you should call her and ask her if she's in the storage units. Don't make me miss school for your funeral because you were killed by an axe murderer. I need the grades."

She did not need ideas like that in her head. "Cookie, you are not helping."

"Three different channels have slasher movie marathons on from now till the thirty-first. I can't help it."

"That's it. You can only watch PBS from now on."

"I'm helping to keep you safe." Jordan pointed at her phone. "Text Lucy."

L, are you in storage 102 bc somebody is and they didn't answer so I called Aaron for backup.

She felt even stupider after she sent the text. Lucy was going to think she was an idiot.

Just home. In parking lot. Was w Roy. Who's in basement?

This was much better and much worse.

Don't know. A says don't go look. Stay away. U 2.

I can keep an eye on back door from my car. Tell A.

This was not good.

Doors locked and engine running?

Brooke got a "thumbs-up" emoji as a response. It would have to do. If anything went sideways, Lucy could have a clean getaway.

Jordan breathed in her ear as she read her phone

screen over her shoulder. Brooke knew who it was and still let out a short squeak.

"That's good, Mom. Now we wait."

For all her daughter's looks were from her father's side of the family, Jordan's personality was a carbon copy of Brooke's, down to her lack of patience. She lasted four minutes on the clock before she checked her phone. "What's taking him so long to get here?"

"The inability to teleport, Cookie."

Eight minutes after her texts to Lucy, Brooke and Jordan were staked out at the living room window, waiting for Aaron to pull up. At twelve minutes, Brooke let her hand hover over her phone. "Should I text him? I'm going to text him."

It chimed as her fingers made contact with the screen. This time, they both jumped. "He's in the parking lot. Lucy's letting him in through the back door to the basement," she read to Jordan. That particular door was a fire exit and was only accessible from the inside unless you had a key, which Lucy did.

"Can't we go to the landing and watch to see who he comes out with?" Jordan asked.

"No, Aaron said to stay inside." Being a good role model sucked. If Jordan had been at work, Brooke had no doubt she'd be staked out in the stairwell, peeking through the railings like a kid looking for Santa on Christmas Eve.

"Can we open the door with the chain on and listen?"

"No. We wait."

Even knowing what was happening, they couldn't hear anything from two floors away. But they didn't need to wait long.

"Mom, look!" A large figure burst through the front door, raced down the street, and cut between two bungalows. Those houses backed onto another residential street. Behind that was Main Street. Another person chased him despite the first person's large head start.

Aaron was no slouch; he was in top physical condition. But he was also over forty, and the form he was after moved like someone half his age. The chasee was also motivated not to get caught, which added to their speed. When Aaron needed a second attempt to clear the fence between the houses, Brooke knew he'd lost the race.

She gave him credit for continuing the pursuit but wasn't surprised to see him return empty-handed. He rounded the corner via the sidewalk with his heavy flashlight in hand. Even at that distance, she saw the frown on his face.

When he reached the apartment building, he looked up. Brooke stepped closer to the window so he could see her. She pointed at herself, then down, asking to join him.

Aaron nodded once.

"I think I'll stay here," Jordan said. "You'll fill me in, right?"

"All the necessary details," Brooke promised. She raced down the stairs and outside.

"You were right. Somebody was hiding in there," Aaron told her when she arrived.

"Did you see who it was?"

"I didn't see his face. I'm sure it was a male, but between the gloves and the hoodie, I don't have a description except for approximate height and weight."

She followed him to the basement. The door to the storage unit was ajar. A sleeping bag lay on the concrete floor. Aside from that, it was empty. "Was he living here?"

"He was fixing to, by the looks of it," Aaron said.

"There's no bathroom."

"There's a utility sink in the laundry room, and Lucy says it's not locked."

"Ew." That was a hard way to live. The basement was dry and heated, but nobody would choose that if they had the slightest opportunity at anything better. Brooke cocked her head and took another look. The storage unit was *completely* empty. There wasn't even any garbage: not a candy bar wrapper, not a drink can, nothing. "He was very careful. Very clean. Very respectful of the property. If he'd managed to get out with his sleeping bag, we would never have known he was here." Which was a worrying thought in itself. What if he had been in here before?

Aaron caught her eyes and held them. "Don't go there. You'll freak yourself out. Like you said, he hadn't had time to make a mess. He hasn't been in there long. You noticed him on your second trip to the laundry room. There are, what, ten families in this building who are in and out all the time? Somebody else would have discovered him long before now."

"Sheriff Gillespie, are you still here?" Lucy called.

"Yes, with Brooke."

The sandy-haired woman appeared at the end the corridor. "Sorry for the delay. I'm still working on contacts in the area. There is a twenty-four-hour locksmith, but he charges triple for calls after eleven o'clock. I can either switch five locks now or fifteen after eight o'clock tomorrow morning. The fire door is locked from the outside. I'll drag a chair into the lobby and wait till morning."

"Lucy, you'll be exhausted."

"I'm also my own boss, so I can give myself tomorrow afternoon off for a nap after the locks are changed. All twelve storage room locks, the front door, fire door, and a new lock for the laundry room door. Just in case."

"I can have whoever is on duty swing by a couple times during the night," Aaron offered.

"I'd appreciate it. In the meantime, I'm going to change into comfy clothes and bring enough snacks and books to make it through my stakeout." She grinned. "Technically it's guard duty, but I'm going to treat it like a stakeout. I'll bring mysteries to make it feel like I'm doing research. Then I can add night watchman to my resumé."

That was one of the reasons she and Lucy were friends, Brooke thought. Only a fellow goofball would find something positive about being forced to stay up all night until a locksmith could show up. At least Lucy's boyfriend—or her soon-to-be fiancé if Brooke was reading things right—would also be working for most of the night. Roy would be at the Escape Room, but she would have someone to talk to until the wee hours of the morning when he shut the bar down. He might even join her. Lucy was pretty lucky, like her nickname.

Brooke wanted that. Then again, she had something pretty close. To call a man in a panic and have him drop everything and come over to make sure she was okay— that was something special. And she knew Aaron would have done it even if he didn't have a badge.

She wasn't doing bad on the luck scale herself.

CHAPTER 25

IT WASN'T OFTEN that their schedules aligned so well. Trevor was at his mother's house for the weekend, while Jordan was with her father. Brooke had all of Sunday off. Aaron had invited her to his place for a meal that didn't require her to be the one doing the home cooking, so she'd jumped on the offer.

Brooke was glad she brought a sweater. Aaron flicked the gas fireplace to life when she arrived, but it wasn't doing much. Not when he was constantly opening and closing the French door to the deck as he checked on the pork chops and vegetable basket he had on the grill. Fortunately, dancing along to the sixties music channel playing on the television helped keep her warm.

She'd contributed the flowers in the vase on the counter. The rest of the festive table setup was all Aaron. Placemats and matching napkins were at each setting. The bottle of wine was already open, and Aaron had poured her a glass while she waited for dinner to be ready. A small plastic jack-o'-lantern pail was in the middle, piled high with Halloween treats.

"No candy before dinner," he teased as he raced past to grab the oven mitt sitting on the counter. "I'm almost ready if you'll pull the salad out of the fridge."

She found a place to set the stainless steel bowl on the table. Aaron brushed by her again, a tray in one hand and a plate in the other. He returned to pull her chair out for her, and he dropped a kiss on her cheek as she took her seat. "Are you prepared for pork chops, grilled vegetables, and potatoes Gillespie?" he asked.

"I don't know what potatoes Gillespie are, but I'm ready to try them."

They turned out to be roughly chopped potatoes, tossed with olive oil, paprika, oregano, and a dash of chili powder. The grilled vegetables were peppers, onions, and whole white button mushrooms. Lastly were thick cut pork chops slathered with barbecue sauce. It was a simple meal but a very tasty one.

When he offered her the last of the potatoes, Brooke had to decline. "I'm too stuffed for one more bite. It was all delicious."

"You can't be too full for dessert. Nobody else is going to eat all those Red Vines."

"Oh, there's always room for licorice," she said with a laugh.

Aaron poured her another half glass of wine, and they moved to the living room where they could enjoy the fire from his sofa. For once, they'd had three uneventful days in a row, and they were luxuriating in the lack of urgency. Brooke was even current on her homework, which was probably why her brain was ready with an answer when Aaron asked a very innocuous question.

"We need an encore for the next open mike night at the Escape Room. What do you think we should do?"

They'd missed the last one; the first Monday of October, she'd had her class, and Aaron had been called out to a car crash. Aaron had mentioned it before that they'd lost their karaoke crowns, but she thought he was joking.

Apparently not.

"It can't be too challenging, because my range isn't great. Or too sad. I refuse to sing a sad song," she said.

"And not Journey again. I hate repeating myself."

"No Beatles," she insisted.

"No Elvis," he countered.

"No boy bands. I can't hit some of those high notes."

"No Spice Girls."

"Mamas and Papas?" she threw out as a suggestion.

Aaron made a wiggle-waggle motion with his hand. "They aren't terrible."

That's when inspiration hit. Brooke put a finger to her lips, then touched her ear. When the confused look didn't leave his face, she pointed at the bar speaker in front of the television. "Listen," she said.

The unmistakable duet singing about being yours to hold your hand and being yours to understand drifted across the room.

A grin crossed Aaron's face. "That has possibilities."

An even bigger grin stretched her cheeks till they hurt. "I have the best idea," Brooke announced. It was fantastic. "It's a shame it'll be after Halloween, but we could still do it."

"Oh, no."

"Trust me, it'll be fun!" The more she thought about it, the more she liked it. "Not only do we do 'I've Got You, Babe,' but we do it in reverse costume."

"*Reverse* costume? So I'd be..."

"Yes! I'll wear my bright yellow T-shirt and a set of

round sunglasses and be Sonny. You wear your hat and be the Cher-iff. Get it?"

Aaron groaned. "That's horrible."

"Horrible and wonderful and memorable. Do you have anything with sequins? They'll have to give us our crowns back," she crowed.

"I'm terrified and intrigued at the possibility."

She pounced on him and kissed him for recognizing her brilliance. "You print out the lyrics. I'll get a copy of the song. Then we'll knock 'em dead in November." She hummed a couple bars, then collapsed into Aaron's chest in a fit of giggles. "This will be epic."

"That'll be one word for it."

Brooke should have known that they'd never get through an entire date without a crime interrupting the evening. She assumed Aaron would be the one to hear about it.

Aaron was doing dishes and she was supervising when she heard a door creak. Brooke knew that door entered from the garage, but she hadn't heard the garage door go up. A teenaged voice called, "Dad, I'm home."

"Okay, son. Brooke and I are in the kitchen."

"Enjoy the rest of your night. I'm going to my room."

"I'll say goodnight later, Trev."

With the snuggle mood interrupted, Brooke excused herself to take advantage of the powder room off the laundry-slash-mudroom where Trevor was. He was still there, emptying the dryer into a basket. She thought nothing of it until he pulled out a beach towel sporting a familiar orange-and-black striped tiger in a blue speedo.

"Trevor, where did you get that?"

He looked at the towel in his hand, then turned white. "This old thing? We've had it forever."

She heard Aaron whistling as he splashed in the kitchen sink. She stepped closer. "Do you want to try again?"

"Really, it's our towel."

"Trevor, I've seen that before. I washed it when we took it from Shelley's Shack after we were stranded there. How did you get it?" she asked quietly.

"I didn't steal it."

"Then how did you get it?" She didn't want to know the answer, but she was the adult in the situation, and she was obliged to ask.

"It's not mine."

"Trevor..."

"It's Caleb's. He usually does his laundry here when he stays over on Friday night, but I was away this weekend and he really needed it done right away so I added it to mine. I was going to give it back to him tomorrow."

"Where did Caleb get it? Did he steal it?"

"No!" The firm denial let a little air back into her lungs. "His parents left it for him when they moved to Vegas."

"Is that what happened?" It explained why neither Lucy nor Aaron couldn't find any sign of them.

"Yeah, back during the summer. They moved out and left him the apartment and a couple pieces of furniture. They said he was eighteen and on his own now."

Pieces started to fall into place. "Lucy said that lease expired at the end of September. Where is he staying now?" *Please don't say Shelley's Shack, please don't say Shelley's Shack,* she chanted in her head.

"Here and there." Brooke didn't have to prompt him again. Trevor looked away when she stared him in the eye. "He stays in his car mostly. Since he got the job at By the Cup, he's been saving for a new place. I invite him over as many Fridays as I can, but I couldn't invite him to Mom's place. At least here he could shower and do his laundry and get a hot supper."

"What about the rest of the time? Because, like I said, I've seen that towel before."

"When you and Dad broke into the cabin, you said it was okay because it was an emergency. Are you the only ones who are allowed to have emergencies?"

"Trees were crashing down around us and could have killed us. We stayed there a few hours, and then repaired and replaced what we used."

"This is the same thing," Trevor insisted. Then the dam broke. "Caleb has fixed that place up. The roof used to leak like crazy, but he's been repairing it as much as he can. He's like a caretaker. Besides, it's not like the Pineys have complained about him being there. They haven't been out all summer. If they don't come on Friday for the weekend, he moves back in and does more repairs during the week. There isn't any power or water so he isn't costing them any money. They don't care. I mean, when those morons threw a party and trashed the place, they still didn't come out to check on the property. Even Dad says they're neglectful. What's the harm?"

"Oh, Trevor." His intentions were coming from a good place, but it didn't make his actions right. There was no good answer for the situation Caleb was in. She couldn't invite the other kid into her apartment; she didn't know him that well, and she and Jordan didn't have the space. Aaron did, but again, inviting a virtual stranger to stay under your roof was a huge step.

"Please don't tell my dad. Caleb hasn't been back

there since the party at Austen Cottage. He's mostly living in his car. He almost has enough money for a security deposit, and he can afford rent now. He won't go back, I promise."

"Living in his car is dangerous. It's getting so cold at night." Another thought came to mind. "Was he the person who was in the storage locker the other night? Did he sneak into my apartment building?"

"Just for that one day."

"That's not okay, Trevor!" There were a dozen different threads sticking out of this messy ball of problems. Brooke didn't have the ability to weave them all back together. "There's a shelter down in Bixby. It operates out of the basement of the First Mission Church. They're good people. Tell Caleb I expect his butt to be there tomorrow night."

"If he does, do you promise you won't tell my dad?" Caleb pressed.

"Do you know what kind of position you're putting me in?" Brooke demanded. It was hard to keep her voice down. "You had knowledge of a crime, and now I do. I can't keep this from Aaron, Trevor. Not just because he's the sheriff, but because he's your dad. I get that Caleb is your friend and you want to help him, but this isn't the way. It also isn't something a teenager should have to worry about. You know that. You bring situations like these to adults and let them deal with it because it's their job."

"He won't do it again, I promise."

"Tell him to go to the shelter. I can give him a day or two to get his act together, but I have to tell your dad. At the very least, he'll stop running himself ragged looking for the person who was in our basement." It was a terrible compromise for everybody, but Brooke couldn't simply throw Trevor and Caleb under the bus. Despite the fact that it sounded like the boys had been working too hard to solve an unsolvable problem, she couldn't keep it a secret forever.

"Fine." The reluctant agreement was loaded with all kinds of attitude, but it was about what she expected. Trevor grabbed the laundry basket. "Night, Dad!" he yelled in the direction of the kitchen.

When Brooke returned to her wineglass, the mood was completely broken. She pasted a smile on her face, but Aaron saw right through it. "What happened? You were only gone for a couple minutes?"

"It's nothing you did. I got some disturbing news," she admitted.

"Do you want to talk about it?"

"I'll let you know in a couple days, okay?"

"That's fine. I'm here whenever you want to talk."

Brooke walked right into the hug he offered. It felt amazing to have somebody to lean on, who wanted to hear about her problems. She'd gone it alone for a long time. Every day, Aaron seemed to give her more of what she didn't know she needed.

She hoped that what she had to do wouldn't change that.

CHAPTER 26

THE HOUSE WAS BLESSEDLY QUIET. Trevor had left for school in a rush of toaster strudels and guzzled orange juice. Aaron cracked the window over the sink as he rinsed his coffee mug. The trees in the backyard only had a couple of green leaves left. Most were yellow or brown, or already on the ground, leaving bare branches waving against the hazy blue sky.

The air was cool, and a light coating of frost covered his windshield. The air also held a touch of wood smoke. It was getting to be that time of year when people with wood burning furnaces would stoke them to keep the chill out of the air overnight. Aaron loved the smell of a good fire.

He was just filling his travel mug when his cell phone rang. Annoyed that they couldn't wait another fifteen minutes for him to get to the station, he answered with a gruff, "Gillespie, what is your emergency?" Because if they were calling before his second cup of coffee, it had better be an emergency.

"Sheriff, it's Gary." Gary Mitchell was the chief of the

Holiday Beach Fire Department. He was one of eight paid firefighters, and he oversaw the volunteers that made up the rest of the department. "We've got a fire. Looks pretty bad."

All of a sudden, Aaron didn't need the coffee to get his heart going. "Where?"

"Shakespeare Drive. The old Shelley's Shack. Someone spotted it on their drive to work and called it in. We're here now, and...we're not going to be able to save it."

"I understand, Chief."

"We're trying to contain it. The grounds aren't well-kept. There's a lot of dead underbrush. There isn't much wind, but it is blowing to the lot to the north."

"That's Bob Mackenzie's place. Mac. He's been working on it."

"Can you contact him? We also need somebody out here directing traffic."

"I'll be there in twenty. Less," Aaron promised.

The fire department had erected a temporary barricade a few lots down from the fire, in front of the Dickens Estate, leaving space for any cars to make a U-turn and head back to Lakeside Drive.

Aaron parked his cruiser in the middle of the road in the other direction. Smoke billowed from behind the trees lining the road. From what he could see, flames only danced higher than the treetops in one location—from where the cottage would be.

He hung back at the pumper truck, not wanting to disturb the men and women at work. His part came after the danger was over. It was almost an hour before Chief Mitchell came over, stripping off his soot-stained jacket. "I think we got lucky. We kept it to the cabin. Some of the trees got a little scorched, but it's under control. The team will go over the scene again to make sure nothing's left to flare up, but between that and the rain we're supposed to get this afternoon, I'm not foreseeing any problems."

"That's good. Everybody is okay on your end?" Aaron asked.

"No injuries. Not even a scratch. We had a close call, but nobody will be complaining the next time I set more training. It really paid off today," the soot-covered man said.

"Can I come up?" Aaron asked. "I need to know if it was an accident or intentionally set."

"I can tell you that. The front door was forced open when we got here, and there was a barbecue full of briquets on its side on the living room floor. Maybe they were trying to use it to stay warm after they broke in. Maybe they had the munchies after a party. I don't know. Nobody was here when we arrived and there were no vehicles around. The rest is up to you."

"You've given me enough to start with. Thanks," Aaron said.

He'd known the abandoned cabin was going to attract more problems. This was the last time he'd have to deal with it, though. Aside from a couple timbers still standing, it had collapsed in on itself and was now a smouldering wreck. It wouldn't host any more parties. Or offer any more shelter to desperate travellers.

Just because the arsonists hadn't been found at the scene of the crime, it didn't mean they had escaped without a trace. Aaron made the rounds of nearby proper-ties, but as he expected, most were empty for the season.

He got a lead at Hemingway's Hideaway. The owners had come out from the city as part of an artists' retreat. The night owls had seen something.

"Sure, there's been a lot of traffic," Antonio Soto-Rojas said. "There's a young man with a pickup truck that's been working in the vacant lot diagonal to us across the road. He's mostly been clearing brush. He and some others constructed some kind of shed on the weekend."

"That's Bob Mackenzie. He bought the property and plans to build there next year," Aaron told them, mostly to put their minds at ease if they saw Mac again while they were out.

"I'm glad to hear that. We could use some new development around here. I hate to say it, but so long as nobody was hurt, that fire was a blessing. Calling it a shack was a compliment. That old building was an eyesore, and a dangerous one at that."

Aaron nodded. He wanted to agree, but he still had to investigate the fire. "Have you seen anyone around there?"

"You mean the fellow that's been hanging around in that blue Toyota rust-bucket?"

"Could be. Can you tell me a little more about this person?"

The vehicle description sounded familiar. The description of the "not even twenty years old, shaggy, white-blond hair, maroon golf shirt everyday" sealed the deal. Aaron raised his hand to eye level. "About yay high? Skinny?"

"That's the fellow."

"I know the guy. I'll talk to him. Thanks."

"Anytime, Sheriff."

Aaron drummed his fingers on the steering wheel.

This was not good. The car and description matched Caleb Quentin, his son's best friend. After working at Mac's place all autumn, Caleb would know that Shelley's Shack was perpetually empty. Aaron couldn't imagine the young man purposely setting fire to a cabin, but the possibility that he broke in and the fire was an accident was a likely scenario.

But he had to check. He knew the teenager worked full-time at By the Cup, but he didn't know if Caleb was on shift now.

He was lucky. The kid was there, behind the counter that was now covered in small, carved pumpkins. Aaron skirted the yellow caution tape marking the chiselled-out tile on the floor by the door where repairs on the old trip hazard were now underway. Rachel Best gave him a questioning look when he asked to speak to Caleb, but she stepped forward to take his place at the till without hesitation.

"Caleb, when did you get to work today?"

"Ten to six. Five-fifty. I opened today."

"Can anybody vouch for that?"

"The customers can verify I opened the door at six. Some of them might have seen me through the windows before then."

"Can I ask where you were last night?" Aaron asked.

The teenager rocked back on his heels, putting distance between them without stepping away. "Why do you want to know?"

"Did you hear about the fire at Shelley's Shack on Shakespeare Drive?"

"Sure, everybody's been talking about it."

"Your car's been seen in the area."

Caleb immediately went pale, and a flop sweat

appeared on his forehead. "I've been working with Mac out there. Cutting down trees and stuff."

"Hmm," Aaron said noncommittally. The kid had some sense of self-preservation, because he didn't let himself ramble. He was pinching his lips together so hard they were turning white. "So, can you tell me where you were last night?"

"Bixby. I was in Bixby."

"All night? Do you have a place there?" Aaron had run Caleb's name through the computer at the office. His address was still listed as the same apartment block as Brooke and Jordan.

Caleb's shoulders hunched forward, and his whole body sagged. "I was at the Mission Church. They have a shelter in the basement. I'm between places at the moment. They can tell you."

Aaron's heart broke at the news. Caleb was just out of high school; that was no place for a kid. "Where are you parents?"

"Vegas, last I heard," Caleb said. "Once I turned eighteen, they said I was on my own."

Aaron could only handle one problem at once. "I'll talk to the church and confirm you were there last night. Then you'll be in the clear." But he couldn't leave it there. "Is it safe? Clean?"

Caleb's head came up a bit. "Yeah. It's not bad."

"Good." He didn't want to add to the kid's stress, but he had to ask. "What would you say if I asked if you'd been staying at Shelley's Shack over the fall?"

If possible, the kid had turned even paler. "Are you asking?"

Now was his moment of truth. Everything he knew about Caleb said the young man wasn't a troublemaker, just a desperate kid in a bad situation. He hadn't done any harm to anyone that Aaron knew about. And, according to Mac, Caleb had actually done some good and kept the shack standing longer than it would have without his help. Aaron didn't know for certain that the Pineys hadn't hired him to do repairs. Was it really his job to ask?

He had suspicions, but as Brooke had pointed out, suspicions did not a crime make. The very least he could do was make sure there had been a crime before he started grilling potential suspects. "Not at the moment. Stay safe and out of trouble, Caleb."

It was a long drive to the station. His son's friend had been homeless for months, and Aaron hadn't had a clue. He wondered if Trevor had. All the Friday night sleep-overs and the odd request to do a load of laundry a teenager shouldn't have volunteered to do told a story, but Aaron forced himself not to jump to conclusions.

But now he had a burned-out cottage and a homeless kid. The first was his job; the second felt like his responsibility. His options as a sheriff were limited, but he could still act as a private citizen. He needed somewhere to start, and his brain was spinning too fast to pick a place. He knew who'd jump at the chance to help. Brooke was at work, but she had a lunch break coming up.

Can I see you?

Sure. After work?

Thanks. See you then.

Something deep inside of him settled. Brooke had quickly become a rock in his life. Between the two of them, they'd find an answer.

CHAPTER 27

BROOKE NEEDED to sit on the corner of the mattress after making the bed. She was exhausted. Not from work, but from a lack of sleep over the last two nights. The Sunday night scene in the mudroom with Trevor played through her head on a loop. What was she supposed to do? She had to talk to Aaron; she knew that. But she had no idea what she was going to say.

She had chatted with Lucy on Monday night when the building manager delivered all the new keys. Brooke flinched again when she thought of the expense of Caleb's actions, but if he still had keys, who knew how many other people hadn't turned theirs in either. The security upgrade wasn't a bad thing.

Lucy mentioned that there was still a waiting list for the two-bedroom units. When Brooke asked about the bachelor apartments, Lucy made a face. "Are you looking to downsize when Jordan goes to college?"

"Not me. A friend might be interested. Is one available?" The tiny suites were beside the manager's office in each building. The bachelor suites took up the rest of the floorplan to match the two-bedroom suites on the upper floors.

"They're all empty. The previous unit manager really let those slide. The more they stood empty, the less he worked on them, and the more they deteriorated. They're all liveable, but none of them are nice. Honestly, I haven't touched them either, although Charlie and Josie have discussed giving me a small budget for them. They need a complete overhaul."

"I might know somebody who'd take one as-is, especially if it came with a discount since it'll be the last one you work on," Brooke said, thinking Caleb needed a cheap place. Safe and clean and worn was better than what he had.

"Some rent coming in for them would be better than the nothing I'm collecting now. If your friend wants a viewing, let me know."

Now all Brooke had to do was talk to Caleb, gently inform him that she knew he was staying in his car, and let him know that she had an apartment he might be interested in without knowing how much he could afford. Easy-peasy. Then she'd spend the afternoon solving world hunger.

When Aaron asked her if she wanted to take a walk down Main Street, she knew something was up. He'd asked her to meet him during the gap between the end of her workday and her study group, so it was important, but it definitely wasn't a date.

The thick frost from the last couple mornings had burned off, but the late fall weather was there to stay. The ground was littered with leaves, and stark, bare branches added atmosphere to the spooky time of year. The sun was already casting long shadows when Brooke met with Aaron.

"You look like you've had a long day," she observed after their first two silent blocks.

"A day and a half, more like it," Aaron said with a sigh. "The good news is I won't have any more callouts to Shelley's Shack for parties or intruders. The bad news is because it burned to the ground yesterday morning."

Everybody had heard there was a fire, but there were few details outside of "on Shakespeare Drive," and the fire crew had done a good job at keeping people away from the scene. She hadn't expected to hear the entire structure was gone. "To the ground?" she repeated. "Was anybody hurt?"

"Thankfully, no. Also, yes, it's all gone. It's a mess. It was also deliberate."

Brooke felt her jaw drop. "Arson? For sure? Do you have any suspects?" She didn't know if he could tell her, but news of a criminal on the loose in Holiday Beach was scary.

"Not at the moment. I had one lead, but it didn't pan out." Aaron took her arm and guided her to the empty playground beside Schultz Middle School. "Trevor's friend, Caleb."

All of a sudden, she felt a knot form in her stomach. "He works at By the Cup with Jordan. You don't think he..."

"His car has been seen in the area lately, so I had to talk to him. He had an alibi. Did you know he was staying at the homeless shelter over in Bixby?"

Her shoulders slumped in relief. Trevor had passed along her request, and more importantly, Caleb had listened to it.

"You did know," Aaron exclaimed. "You were right. You have absolutely no poker face."

"I heard about his situation a couple of days ago. I tried to get word to him that the Mission Church had a shelter to help people who were down on their luck. I wasn't even sure he got the message. I'm awfully glad he checked it out." He'd gone there just in time, by the sounds of it. She couldn't imagine the terror of needing an alibi during an arson investigation. "But you're sure it wasn't him, right?" Trevor would be devastated if his friend ended up under suspicion.

"He's in the clear. But if you knew, and you knew he was Trevor's friend, why didn't you tell me? You know that Lucy asked me to track down his family at the beginning of September. It explains why I couldn't find any sign of them. How long have you known?"

"When I said I found out a couple of days ago, I literally meant two days. I found out and have been working on finding him a place to stay. I spoke to Lucy today, and I have another place on my list," she explained. "You have to know that the situation isn't easy."

"You should have told me," he insisted, his hot words blowing out a cloud of steam when he spoke.

"Remember on Sunday night, when I said I got some difficult news and needed a day or two to get my head around it? This was it, Aaron. I'm doing my best here. Your son's friend is homeless. How can we help him?"

His next sigh wasn't aimed at her. "Protect and serve is in the job description, but solving problems like this is beyond the scope of the badge. I wish I'd known earlier, though. I could have done something. Not officially, but personally."

"I know that. We're both worried. You have been

helping, even if you didn't know it. All those Fridays that you let Caleb sleep over, even when you were tired of the extra person in the house. You gave him a chance to have a roof over his head. You gave him a hot meal. You let him shower and do all his laundry."

Aaron had been nodding along as she'd listed everything that he'd already done without realizing it. Until she hit the last item on her list. "What? He didn't do *all* his laundry at our place," he said.

"Didn't you tell me he was constantly draining your hot water tank?" she hedged. She was certain he'd said something similar.

"I said shower." He stared into her eyes. "Has Caleb been doing all laundry at my house? I knew there was a couple of loads. How could you even know that it was his?"

She should have stopped while she was ahead, but she wasn't going to lie. "I saw Trevor with some stuff."

"But how do you know it was Caleb's? He and Trevor are about the same size."

"You don't seem like the type to have cartoon tiger towels."

"We aren't." Aaron fell silent. For two very long minutes. "But I know where I could find some if I wanted them. We used tiger towels when we were stranded in Shelley's Shack. You took them home to wash them after the fact."

Busted.

"Which means Caleb was at the cabin," he continued.

"He could have been there. Maybe. The towels looked like they were from the dollar store, though. I'm sure they weren't the only ones in town."

"You knew." It wasn't quite an accusation. It didn't have the tone.

But it was too close for comfort. "I realized it was possible, but I didn't have any proof. I haven't talked to him in person aside from giving him my order at By the Cup."

"Brooke, you suspected, and you didn't tell me."

"Aaron, I told you that I found out he was homeless on Sunday. Today is Tuesday. So far, I've gotten him into a shelter and possibly found a cheap studio apartment he can rent. What else do you expect from me?" She wasn't Super Girl. She wasn't even Semi-Super Girl.

"You knew about a crime. I expected that you would tell me, your boyfriend the sheriff, about it."

"I'd be worse than Neil Dempsey if I'd said anything. Not only do I not have any proof a crime was committed, but I would also be pinning a target on Caleb's back! I never saw him at Shelley's Shack. I have no proof the towels in the cabin were his. There is no cabin anymore, so any proof he was ever there is gone anyway. All you have is proof that he wasn't the person who set the fire."

"Brooke, you're reaching."

"If he was there, do you have proof that he didn't have permission from the owners? They haven't called you back about pressing charges for the partiers, and that crew caused all kinds of property damage. For all you know, Caleb had permission to stay there—not that I'm saying he *was* there. Because I don't know. And neither do you."

"What are the odds of that?"

"I have no idea. What I do know is that if we broke into that place for emergency shelter and the owners didn't care—and since they never got back to you, I think that's a fair assessment—I shouldn't assume they'd care if Caleb did the same thing."

Her arguments weren't convincing him. "You should have told me, Brooke. You've put me in a real predicament."

"Welcome to my life. Now we both have secondhand information, we have no proof of anything, and we still have a teenager with no place to go." Brooke had been right the first time. There was no right answer to this situation. There were just shades of horrible choices, and she'd made the best one she could. Now it was Aaron's turn.

"I need to go. I have to deal with..." He swung his hand around, as if he could encompass the entire situation with one easy move.

"As the sheriff?" she asked. "Or as Trevor's dad? I can work with Trevor's dad on trying to help, but I can't help the sheriff."

He didn't answer. He also didn't kiss her goodbye when he left.

CHAPTER 28

THE FIRE WAS long out but his temper was still blazing. Aaron changed into his rubber fishing boots and slowly made his way around the burnt-out shell of the cabin. He told himself that he wasn't going to find any sign Caleb had been in the area, but he looked around anyway.

There was nothing there. The dry, rotting timbers in the roof had gone up like kindling, as had the rest of the wooden structure. There wasn't even much left to be cleaned up. The appliances needed to be removed but, sadly, everything that was left would fit into a couple of dump trucks.

He heard snapping branches and muttered grunts coming from the bush behind him. A moment later, Mac Mackenzie stumbled into view. The ash-streaked painter puffed out a greeting. "I thought you might be the arsonist returning to the scene of the crime," Mac said. He squinted at Aaron. "You aren't, are you?" he joked.

"Very funny."

"I know it's serious, but what is funny is that whoever

did it actually did me a favor. Did all of us along this stretch one. We're lucky the fire was contained, but by removing this eyesore, it may have increased our property values. Who knows—maybe the Pineys will finally sell the land now that their only reason to come to Holiday Beach is gone," Mac said.

"Are you saying the land is worth more without the cottage on it?" Aaron asked. That added a new angle to the arson investigation.

"That'll be up to the insurance adjustors, but I wouldn't be surprised." Mac stepped back and took in the entire clearing. "Man, we got lucky. If the boys and I hadn't cleared so much deadfall out of the brush as we did, the rain wouldn't have helped so much." He pointed to some scorched saplings along the path coming from his place. "We pulled four full-length logs from in there. Can you imagine what would have happened if they'd been there to catch fire?"

"We got very lucky."

"Do you think Joe Piney will want to sell? Because I'd be interested in getting this property too."

"I'll let you know if I ever get a hold of anybody," Aaron griped. He still hadn't had a single returned call from any of the contact numbers he'd been able to find. He'd been calling Joe Piney for three days straight to inform him about the loss of their cabin. Not even his son Gerald had bothered to call him back. If they didn't respond by the end of the day, he was calling in favors with some police friends in Minneapolis and sending them to knock on doors until he got a response.

"Are you sure you haven't seen anybody hanging around who shouldn't be here?" Aaron asked. Mac worked with his younger sibling Doug at Mackenzie

Brothers Painting. Aaron knew that kept him busy during the week, which was why Mac had only needed help from Trevor and Caleb on weekends. If he'd had a short day or some free evenings, he might have spent it on his property and seen something without realizing the significance.

"Not really. I missed the party from a couple weekends back. I saw the Soto-Rojas today, so I know they're around, but other than it's been very quiet. It always is this time of year. Seeing anybody on this stretch is memorable."

That didn't help at all. "What about Caleb Quentin?"

"Well, obviously he's been around. He was staying here for a while, doing repairs. I guess he finished a couple weeks ago because I haven't seen him since."

"Are you positive?"

"Yes. The kid got a bum deal if you ask me. I hope he negotiated a better arrangement for his next place. The Pineys didn't even leave the electricity on for him. He stayed here during the week. I saw him on the roof, patching spots and replacing shingles that blew off. It was pretty ballsy considering the shape of the roof. He patched some of the siding, got the worst of the deadfall away from the house, and chopped it into firewood. Not that you can tell now." Mac gestured at the black spot where the woodpile had once stood.

"Are you saying the Pineys knew he was here?"

Mac shrugged. "I assume so. If he wasn't, nobody cared enough to tell him to leave. Was he not here with permission?"

Now Aaron didn't know what to think. Until the Pineys bothered to return a call, he didn't know anything.

"Do you know where Caleb is now? I haven't seen him in a while," Mac continued.

"He's staying at the Mission church shelter over in Bixby."

Mac swore. "I wish I'd known. I could have found some hours for him, here or with me and Doug. How did you find out he was staying in Bixby?"

"Brooke told me he was sleeping in his car."

"She knew? And she didn't do anything? That doesn't sound like her."

The painter had a point. "She just found out. She's been trying to find him a cheap place to stay."

"That sounds more like it. Did she ask you for help?"

"She didn't tell me. She knew Caleb was squatting here, and she didn't breathe a word."

"Did you want her to tell you-you or sheriff-you?"

What an odd question. "What do you mean? I am always the sheriff."

"Maybe that's why."

People kept telling him that, but he was who he was. "I'm also Trevor's father. She knows he's been hanging out with Caleb. Caleb has spent just as many Friday nights at my place as Trevor has this fall. She should have said something."

"I thought you said she just found out."

"On the weekend," Aaron admitted.

"You'd better make up your mind. Holding on to information like that for two days isn't a crime."

"I'm just trying to do my job, Mac."

"She's not stopping you from doing that. Maybe she was just trying to find a way to solve the problem without calling in the cops. No offense. Is it a crime to try to give yourself a little wiggle room to get out of a situation? Maybe she thought Caleb had permission, like I did."

"She didn't. She told me so."

"You might want to think like someone who isn't a cop and who has never played one on television. Whatever she thought, I assume she had no evidence that an actual crime was committed. She did know a teenager, your son's friend, was in trouble and tried to help before involving you as a parent and as the sheriff. What would you have done in her shoes?"

Would Aaron have gone running to her with accusations of a potentially imaginary crime, pointing the finger at a child who was barely legal? Especially after witnessing Neil Dempsey's repeated attempts to get him to find a patsy to blame for unproven, minor wrongdoings? Would he have assumed the best of her child's friend and tried to help, or thought the worst of him?

He used to be the type of man who'd help first. He never used to reach for the handcuffs first and ask questions later. Perhaps Brooke had been right during the conversation they'd had long before the fire. Maybe he was so burned out on being a police officer that he'd forgotten how not to be one, even when it came to his own son and girlfriend. "You know, I'm not a bad cop. I do my job well."

Mac gave him a disappointed look. "That's not the question, Aaron. I think you know that."

CHAPTER 29

BROOKE'S EARS ached at the squeal of tires as her car screeched to a stop inches from the big red mailbox on the corner. She closed her eyes when a bright yellow VW bug skidded toward her front bumper, then opened one cautiously when she didn't feel an impact. Emily Handler looked at her with wide eyes through the windshield.

Up the street, Helen Pham wasn't as lucky. The navy, extended cab pickup that Brooke had narrowly avoided had glanced off the passenger side of Helen's SUV and bounced her into a street light.

Brooke turned off the engine and reached for her purse, which had slipped off the seat beside her and ended up on the floor.

Despite how mad Aaron was at her, she had no doubt the person she was calling would answer the phone. "I need your help, Aaron."

"What's wrong, Brooke?"

"Neil Dempsey's son is heading north on Main Street." She watched the pickup swerve into oncoming traffic at the three-way stop sign on the corner. "Now he's heading north on Lakeside Drive. He almost hit at least two cars, and he hit Helen Pham for sure. He dropped a bottle in the liquor store parking lot, and from the glaze in his eyes when he drove by, he was already topped off."

"Do you need an ambulance on scene?"

Brooke looked at the crowd gathering around the SUV. "I'm not sure yet. I'll call for one if we do. Can you stop Ryan before he hurts anyone else?"

"I'm on it. I'll call in for backup."

"Don't let him hurt you either. He's driving like a maniac."

"I won't." He went silent for a moment. "I've got to go."

"Please call me later," she said. But he was already gone.

That could have gone better, she said to herself. She expected the brusque tone. Aaron had not been thrilled with the way she'd handled the Caleb situation. He had a tiny point when it came to her sharing that information with him as Trevor's father; she understood where that came from. What was really unfair was that he was mad as a Holiday Beach sheriff. On that front, she didn't feel guilty at all. He was one to talk about trust. If she'd known for sure a serious crime was going on, she would have reported it, but he'd already convicted her on his opinion of what he assumed had happened.

She took a breath, then waved at Emily to back up. Once the Bug was safely back on the proper side of the street, Brooke pulled forward until she was in an actual parking spot. Then she got out and went to check on the other accident victims.

"Do you need an ambulance, Helen?"

"No, I'm mobile. I'm going to have to see my doctor,

though." The short Asian woman winced when she looked over her shoulder into the back seat. "I'm very grateful I was on my way to pick up Shelly at school instead of being on my way home with her in the back. Was that Ryan Dempsey behind the wheel? I think he toasted me with a bottle of scotch."

"I'm not going to comment, but I encourage you to report what you saw, or think you saw, to the sheriff when he gets here." Brooke was already in hot water. She didn't need to make things worse.

"Do you think Sheriff Gillespie will catch them?"

"Absolutely. I've already called him."

Helen pressed the ignition button, but the engine didn't even turn over. "I guess there's no way to drive this to the garage. I'll have to call Tom for a tow."

"I'm sure the police can drive you home," Brooke said as a cruiser pulled up. She let Helen speak to the deputy first, then gave her own statement when Aaron didn't appear. She hung around until the damaged cars had been taken away and the officer was preparing to leave.

"Do you know where Sheriff Gillespie is?" she asked.

"He's back at the station."

"I see. Thanks."

She blinked rapidly as she walked back to her car. That news stung. She thought Aaron would have at least come out to the scene of the accident to see if she was okay. Or called her back to let her know that they'd caught the drunk driver. Or even to say, "Thank you for the tip about the crime in progress, Brooke."

She tried to shake it off. She'd done her duty. She'd been a good citizen and a good friend. The rest was out of her hands.

Brooke thought she'd done a good job of hiding her

irritation, but Jordan cornered her while they were doing dishes. Her little girl was taller than her now, so Brooke had to look up when Jordan said, "You haven't texted with Trevor's dad in a couple days. Is everything okay?"

"We're a little annoyed with each other at the moment, so we're taking some time to cool off." At least, she hoped that was all that was going on. If it was more serious, she trusted Aaron would be an adult and discuss it with her.

After a long minute, Jordan asked, "Are you annoyed because I published the parking lot piece and he had to deal with Marjory Major?"

"What? No, Cookie, this has nothing to do with you." Brooke wrapped her arm around her daughter's shoulder. "I promise. We disagree on how I handled a situation. It's a bigger issue than I first thought, but how we handle this will affect how we handle things in the future, so we need to make sure we find a solution we can both live with."

Jordan squeezed her back. "Or he could just apologize to you," she suggested.

"How do you know I'm not the one who needs to apologize?"

"Because you would have done it already."

"You are, by far, my favorite child."

"I'll remind you of that the next time Principal Kelly calls."

"What? Are you already working on a new story, or do I have the rest of the month off?"

"Mom, it's already the twenty-third. That's not much of a vacation."

"Let me dream, Cookie." It didn't matter if Jordan had a dozen more stories coming out. Brooke pulled her over to kiss her cheek. "You are always the best part of my day. Don't worry about me and Aaron. We'll figure it out."

She decided to give the stubborn man till eight o'clock to call her and update her on the Ryan Dempsey situation, among other things. If he hadn't called by then, she would.

But she didn't have to. Three minutes before the deadline he didn't know he had, Aaron's face appeared on her phone screen. For a brief moment, she considered turning her irritation on him and letting it go to voicemail, but she shook off the thought. Jordan disappeared to her bedroom, leaving Brooke in the living room, moonlight streaming through the window. "Hey there," she said quietly.

"Hey yourself." The line went quiet. "Sorry, I yawned there. How are you? Deputy Sanders said you were okay at the scene, but this is the first chance I've had to check."

The accident had been hours ago. Knowing he'd inquired about her gave him a smidgen of goodwill since he hadn't come to see her. "Are you still at the station?"

"I'm parked outside the house trying to find the energy to make it inside. It's been a very long day."

Brooke swung her feet onto the sofa and pulled the throw blanket over her legs. "Want to tell me about it?"

"I don't know where to start."

"Where were you when I called?" she suggested.

"At Shelley's Shack. Or what's left of it."

"Hmm." She hoped she sounded supportive. The only reason he could be out there was if he was looking for clues for the arsonist. Despite Caleb's alibi, she knew the teen was still Aaron's best suspect.

"I ran into Mac while I was there. He knew Caleb had been staying in the cabin. He was under the impression Caleb had permission to be there. Since the Pineys haven't bothered to call me back yet, I have no reason to think otherwise."

Brooke clenched her teeth together so tightly her jaw ached. That was exactly what she'd said to Aaron, only she'd been dismissed without a thought. "Hmm," she managed to say again.

"I was on my way back to the station when you called, so I was already on Lakeside Drive. I saw Ryan coming. Fortunately, I had time to hit my lights and the two other cars between us managed to pull over before he went screaming past me. By the time I managed to turn around, he'd already plowed off the road, through the guard rail, and into the lake."

"Oh, no," she breathed. The thick metal bands that lined the shoulder along the river were good for marking the edge of the road, but they weren't meant to stand up to that kind of impact. "How was he?"

"Wet, but fine. After we fished him out and were loading him into the ambulance, he asked the EMT to go back and get the rest of his scotch from the front seat because he was thirsty."

"Does that count as a spontaneous admission of guilt?"

"Have you been watching *Law and Order* repeats again?"

"It's research!"

This is where they used to be. Teasing each other. Sharing their days. Brooke could pretend that they were again, but that was ignoring the problem. Sooner or later, they were going to have to talk about it.

"That will be for the judge to decide, but it's not looking good for him."

"I'm glad you got him before he hurt anyone else. I've been thinking of what would have happened if this had been a week from now with all the little trick-or-treaters on the street."

"Now I'm going to have that nightmare." A heavy silence stretched between them. "How's the studying going?" Aaron asked.

Brooke glanced at the textbook on the coffee table beside her. "It's going. My midterm is on Monday."

"That's a big one, right?"

"Thirty percent of my grade."

"I'll let you study then. Have a good night, Brooke."

"You too, Aaron."

Coward! She wasn't sure who that was aimed at—Aaron or herself. Jordan had been right. If she thought she'd been in the wrong, she would have apologized already. She assumed Aaron felt the same. But somebody needed to be the grownup and bring the discussion to the table, and today both of them had fallen down on the job. She'd been so grateful to hear from him that she hadn't wanted to break the mood. Now her eagerness left a sour taste in her mouth.

She stretched and pulled the textbook and highlighter into her lap. She was too upset to sleep now, so she might as well study. She could at least keep that part of her future on track.

CHAPTER 30

PATROLLING WAS SUPPOSED to be mindless. That was why he took the afternoon shift. Aaron cruised Main Street, then along Lakeside Drive, enjoying the sun glinting off the calm water on the lake. The air was cool, but the sky was bright and clear. It was no wonder that he turned the corner to find Gene Wyatt leaning against his backyard fence, rake in hand, taking in the nice afternoon.

"How goes the battle?" Aaron called through the open passenger side window.

"Leaf bags four, oak trees a lot more," came the cheerful reply. "But I'm gaining on them."

Aaron had never known the sprightly, white-haired senior to be caught resting on his laurels. Or even on his front porch. The Wyatts' backyard was an ocean of blooms in the spring and summer. It took them a good month to get it ready for winter. It looked like Gene was halfway there. "Do you need a hand?" Aaron asked.

"No, thanks, Sheriff. Jean mostly wanted me out of the house so she could arrange my birthday supper. She should be back from the grocery store any time now with a couple thick steaks to throw on the grill."

"She's barbecuing you dinner?"

"No, she's baking the potatoes and making the other fixings. The grill is my domain."

"Well, I'll let you get finished here so you can have a nap before your big party."

"Nap? Nap? I've heard this word. I'm pretty sure they're for people without to-do lists."

"Isn't that the truth. Those preschoolers don't know how good they have it," Aaron agreed with a laugh. "Happy birthday, Gene."

"Thanks, Sheriff."

That's what his job was supposed to be like, Aaron thought. Checking on the community. Making sure everyone was doing okay.

Not getting robbed while they were doing yard work and their wives were at the store.

He tapped the brakes as he turned right at the corner. Two young men in their early twenties were walking out the Wyatts' front door, one carrying a medium sized flat-screen television, the other caring a sound system console with a sound bar balanced on top of the black box. Aaron put the cruiser in park at the foot of the driveway, blocking in a battered blue pickup truck with unfamiliar plates.

"Good afternoon. Does Gene know you two are walking his entertainment system out the front door while he's raking leaves in his backyard?" Aaron asked. He was certain that Gene would have said something about giving away several hundred dollars' worth of electronics when he wasn't in the house.

"Of course he does," one of them said. "But we're kinda in a hurry."

"Why would he do that?"

"He was feeling generous," the shorter of the two men said with a smirk.

"Let's verify that theory. I'll go ask Gene, and you two can wait in the back of the cruiser." There was a little satisfaction when the smug look on the fellow's face evaporated. It was replaced with a mix of confusion and anger.

"Are you serious?"

"The badge says I am."

They entered the back of the cruiser, grumbling and sullen, but without a fight. Once the door was closed, they were locked in until he let them out. Aaron couldn't believe the brazenness of their actions. They'd been entirely confident as they walked out of the house. If he hadn't been there... Aaron looked around the neighborhood. At this hour, hardly anybody was around. Most of the folks who worked at home were on their way to the schools to pick up their kids. Those two could have just kept walking away, and nobody would have been the wiser.

"Hey, Gene," Aaron yelled over the fence. "Can you come through to the front door, please?"

"Okay?" Aaron heard the scrape of a metal rake as it rubbed a concrete sidewalk stone. A minute later, the senior opened the door wearing a puzzled look. "Is there a problem, Sheriff?" he asked.

"You didn't happen to give two young fellows permission to take your television and sound bar, did you?"

"You bet I did. Take a look." Gene swept his arm, indicating that Aaron should step inside and head into the living room. A brand-new, larger flatscreen sat on a table, with a new sound system, including a sound bar and a subwoofer, on the shelves underneath. The boxes were still on the floor, Styrofoam corner blocks poking out of the top. "My dear Jean got me a new setup for my birthday. You only turn seventy once. How did you know?"

"I saw two men carrying your television out the front door while you were in the back."

"That's Sean Patrick's nephew. He's bought the old ones for his dorm room."

"Oh."

"Sheriff, is there a problem?"

"It looked suspicious, so I asked them to wait a minute while I verified the situation."

Gene stared at him through his bushy eyebrows. "Where did you ask them to wait?"

"In the back of the cruiser," Aaron admitted. No wonder they were upset. They hadn't done anything wrong. They'd even answered his questions honestly; the smirk had just set off a switch in his brain that made "suspect" flash over the fellow's head.

"Well, let's go let them out and send them on their way," Gene said.

Aaron opened the cruiser door, and the men scrambled out silently. "Mr. Wyatt verified your story. I'll let you finish loading your truck."

The short one remained silent. The other gave him a grudging "Thanks, Sheriff Gillespie."

Aaron put the cruiser in reverse, so they had room to pull out. He stayed in the vehicle while they secured the electronics. Gene shook their hands and clapped them on the shoulder. Both studiously ignored Aaron as they drove away.

Aaron returned to the senior on the porch. "I feel like

I should apologize for that, but it was too suspicious to just let go without checking it out."

"Is there a lot of suspicious activity in Holiday Beach these days, Sheriff?"

"It feels like it." It seemed like everything was a threat these days. Holiday Beach hadn't seen this much off-season crime since he'd been a second-year deputy. With the recent vandals identified and under watch, Aaron expected the callouts to Shakespeare Drive to fall off considerably until it got too cold for people to go out and make trouble.

He still didn't have a solid lead on the arson. He'd asked Poppy, and she couldn't remember the last time the department had to investigate an arson. While his logical brain knew the crime wave was an anomaly, it seemed like his nerves were so tightly wound, he saw everything as another invader attacking his hometown.

"I've heard you've had some action lately. You should take some time off. Relax before you gave yourself an ulcer. A man needs a break," Gene told him, his voice heavy with old man wisdom.

Maybe Gene was right. Maybe he could use a good vacation.

Which meant Brooke was right too. If he couldn't take off his sheriff's hat, he was going to burn out, and then he wouldn't be able to help anybody, including himself. Even worse, the relationships he'd be damaging would be personal ones.

Aaron was running out of time. He had to make some changes. He had too much to lose.

CHAPTER 31

IT WASN'T easy finding a time where she and Lucy were both free that also coincided with Caleb finishing a shift while he wasn't working with Jordan, but with a little help from Rachel Best, they were able to find a twenty-minute gap in all their schedules.

Brooke and Lucy claimed the corner table in By the Cup and waited for Caleb. Brooke had been hesitant to give Lucy all the details, but the conversation would have been impossible otherwise, so she swore her friend to secrecy. Then they got to work.

"Caleb, why don't you join us?" Brooke invited. She recognized the look that flashed across the teenager's face. He was going to make a break for it. "No, I insist. I really do."

Lucy took the lead. The sandy-haired woman solved problems for a living, although most of those were building-related. Brooke trusted her to find a way to make their current life-fixing scheme work. "I don't know if you know this, Caleb, but I'm currently holding on to the damage deposit from your family's apartment."

The kid relaxed slightly when he realized he wasn't in trouble. "I didn't know that."

"I can't release the funds to you, but I could carry them forward as a damage deposit toward a new apartment for a family member, which leads me to my next subject."

Caleb shifted in his chair, his toes pointing to the exit.

"I hear you might be looking for an apartment if the price was right. We haven't rented them in years, but I'm looking at renting one of the studio apartments in the Remington Arms complex as a trial to see if there's a market for them in Holiday Beach. I have to warn you, they are small. They have the same footprint as a two-bedroom unit but over half of the square footage went into the manager's office. You get a full bathroom, a kitchenette wall with a fridge, sink, stove and two feet of countertop, and one room that's for everything else."

His eyes widened at the description. Not in horror at the postage-stamp size suite she described, but in eagerness at the offer.

Lucy held up her hands. "Don't get excited. That's a trial rent for the first six months. There would be no penalty on your end if you decide you want to break the lease early. I cannot overstate this enough—this place is tiny. It's also old. I can clean it and slap a fresh coat of paint on the walls, but it needs an overhaul, which it won't be getting until I can prove to the Franklins that people are willing to live there."

Caleb looked like the deal sounded too good to be true. Brooke knew the feeling. She'd had too many of her own hopes dashed after reality reared its ugly head when she was desperate for a break. It had taken a lot of work to achieve the stability she and Jordan enjoyed now, and she was working hard for something even better. If somebody offered her a lucky opportunity, she'd take it without thinking twice. Happily, she had a cushion to fall back on now.

"How much rent are we talking about?" he asked cautiously.

Brooke was shocked at the ridiculously low number Lucy gave him. Even at the minimum wage Caleb was earning, he'd be able to afford it, with enough left over for groceries and a few extras. "And, as I said, I already have your damage deposit. You could have the place starting November first. Earlier if you offered to help with the painting," Lucy told him.

Considering that it was already the twenty-fourth, that meant Caleb could be settled into his new place in less than a week. Brooke crossed her fingers under the table. *Come on, kid, take the deal.*

"I think that would work."

"Excellent." Lucy stood quickly and grabbed her coffee. "I'll go get started on the paperwork. Come by Building A tomorrow, and we'll get the lease signed. I'll hand over the keys and show you what needs painting. Spoiler, it's everything."

"I have the late shift. Will twelve o'clock work?"

"Sounds good." She clapped a hand on his shoulder as she squeezed by him. "If this works, and I get the other two studio apartments leased as well, the Franklins are going to love me. You could be my lucky charm, Caleb."

Brooke was surprised when he didn't race for the door after Lucy left. He turned to her, then ducked his head. "Trevor said that you recognized my towels. He told me he told you."

"I'm not asking where you were staying. It's probably

better that I don't know for sure. Are you okay at the shelter for a while longer?"

"Yeah. It's warmer than my car. Thanks for the tip."

She nodded.

"This was you, too?" He gestured at Lucy driving by the window.

"I put the bug in her ear that you were looking for a cheap place to rent. Renovating the studios was her idea." It was too late to be delicate now. "Will you be able to afford it?" The whole plan was moot if it was still too expensive for him.

"I can get some more work. Mac Mackenzie said he might have some hours if I can work around my barista schedule." Caleb sat a little straighter on the hard-backed plastic chair. "I'm not afraid of work, Ms. Portman. I just got a little overwhelmed, and then things snowballed."

"You don't owe me an explanation, Caleb. I've been there. Maybe not all the way there, but I've been close. I know what it's like to pay rent and have ten dollars left in your wallet to make it to your next payday. I'm just happy I was able to help a little bit."

"You helped a lot. You didn't have to."

"Us folks in the service industry have to stick together. Can I offer you another tip?" She was loath to do it, but it wasn't about him being embarrassed. It was about offering a hand to someone when she'd been in their shoes. "The Main Street United Church here in Holiday Beach is associated with the Mission Church in Bixby. We operate a food bank out of the basement that's open Wednesday nights and Saturday mornings. We're always looking for more hands, and volunteers can set aside a box at the beginning of their shifts. Sometimes you need the hand, sometimes you can lend one, and sometimes it's both at the same time." Brooke had been on both sides of the equation when she and Denny had just gotten married and were trying to make it with a baby on his salary. She'd never forgotten.

"Thanks, Ms. Portman." He stood to go. "Do you know if Sheriff Gillespie is still asking questions about Shelley's Shack?"

"No, I don't. I would suggest that you not do anything that gets you in trouble for the next little while, until things settle down about the fire."

"That's good advice. He seems like a good guy, but I don't want to get on his bad side."

Brooke shook her head in agreement. "Nobody wants that."

Especially her.

CHAPTER 32

THE FIRST THING Aaron Gillespie needed to do was figure out the first thing he had to do. The problem that Brooke had dropped in his lap—

No. That wasn't fair. She'd had just two days more than him to deal with some very disturbing knowledge. The cabin fire wasn't even a consideration when she'd learned about Caleb Quentin's situation. All Brooke had done was try to be a decent person and help a kid who, from the sounds of it, didn't have anyone else in his corner.

Aaron had done a thorough background check. Caleb's parents were in the wind. After moving out of the Remington Arms in August, they'd vanished. Lucy confirmed that nobody had called to verify their rental references.

As for the kid they'd left behind, the eighteen-year-old was doing well at the coffee shop and was making a livable wage. Unfortunately, he had no place to go because as a brand-new adult, he had no savings and no credit history, which mean any reputable place wouldn't give him a lease, and any unreputable place would be as risky as staying in his car. His options sucked. The shelter would do for now, but Aaron needed to follow up with Brooke about the apartment she'd mentioned. He couldn't do much, but he might be able to help an inexperienced teenager negotiate a lower rent.

Of course, that meant talking to her about something of substance. His pride wasn't ready to do that.

His temper wasn't appeased at Brooke's arguments either. Her point about the owners of Shelley's Shack not being interested in the property was more on point than she knew. Aaron had spent the afternoon on the phone to Minneapolis and had finally got a hold of somebody. But it wasn't any of the Pineys. It was a lawyer for the estate of Joe Piney, Senior.

"What do you mean, you can't confirm if Caleb Quentin had permission to stay at the cabin?" Aaron repeated.

"Joe Senior went into palliative care at the very beginning of the summer and passed away at the beginning of the month. I can't discuss the power of attorney, but suffice it to say that there were some communication difficulties between them, plus the fact that Joe Senior was still making decisions. I have no idea if the young man you're asking about received permission from one or any of them to be on the property at Holiday Beach," the tired-sounding woman said.

"So, Caleb Quentin might have been trespassing, but he also might have had permission, but we'll never be sure?"

"Which answer will generate less paperwork?" she asked.

"Saying he had permission."

"Good, let's go with that."

"What if the family decides that nobody gave Caleb permission? Will they want to press charges for breaking and entering?"

"Absolutely not." It was the first direct answer the lawyer had given him. "Sheriff Gillespie, can I be blunt?"

"It would be appreciated."

"The family isn't interested in pressing charges. Not for the damages caused by the party, not for"—Aaron heard pages shift—"your own breaking and entering. Not if somebody was staying there, with or without permission." The woman at the other end of the call sighed. "Honestly, Sheriff Gillespie, the family is too busy squabbling over the value of the property to do anything with it. Nobody is interested in investing any money in the cabin in case they don't get it back. That place burning to the ground was the best thing that could have happened. Now I can just sell the property and close out this file."

He didn't understand people sometimes. "You want to sell it? You understand that there was a fire there that looked like arson."

"Joe Piney Senior let the insurance lapse on the cabin before he died. The family can't even make a claim for damages. That's probably why nobody's gotten back to you. They're very lucky nobody got hurt."

"The town is going to want someone to pay for the fire crew and all of that."

"If you give me a name, I'll forward them my contact details, but Holiday Beach will probably just have to put a lien on the property and get paid back when it sells."

"What about the potential squatter?"

"If you had any proof there was one, it would have burned in the fire, right?"

"Right," he reluctantly agreed.

"Put the reports in the circular file, Sheriff. Don't spend another minute on them."

Aaron wasn't a lawyer, but he had a feeling that the lawyer's instructions meant Caleb Quentin was in the clear for anything he might have done. Which was good for the kid, frustrating for him professionally, and relieving for him as the father of a teenager who only wanted to help his friend. Besides, the only option he really had was to put pressure on Caleb to see if the kid would confess to being there without permission, but even if Aaron had that information, he couldn't do anything with it.

Was Brooke right? Was he so used to seeing the worst in people that he wasn't able to give anyone the benefit of the doubt? Was he so burned out on the job that he was trying to create cases for himself? This, plus the incident at the Wyatts', certainly gave that impression. Maybe he did need some time off. He couldn't remember the last time he'd taken more than a long weekend for a vacation. There was no good reason for the self-denied privilege.

The very thought of being away from the station churned his guts. That was a sign in itself. He worked with good people, competent law enforcement officers. The whole town wouldn't fall apart if he took a vacation. If he came back relaxed and able to focus, he'd be an even better sheriff.

He owed Brooke a big apology for treating her as a suspect instead of as his girlfriend.

Aaron heaved himself to his feet and moved to the computer in the office. Halloween was just around the corner, but the first week of November was notoriously slow before things started picking up before Thanksgiving. Instead of just taking the afternoon off to take Trevor to Woodlands Trades Institute, there no reason for him not to take an entire week off for some rest and relaxation.

And because it was all Brooke's idea, he'd make sure to share some of that time with her. If she'd still want to.

CHAPTER 33

THE CHARRED HUSK of a building wasn't the most romantic location Brooke could think of, but when Aaron called after another silent weekend and asked if they could talk and suggested the spot, she agreed without hesitation. They needed to have a serious conversation; the place was irrelevant.

But maybe it was more than a convenient spot for him to meet while he was on duty. After she parked on the street and walked up the lane to where Shelley's Shack used to be, she found a card table with a thermos, two mugs, and a plate of baked treats. Folding lawn chairs sat on either side. And Aaron, out of uniform.

The trees were mostly bare, but the spruce and pines blocked most of the breeze coming off the lake. Aaron was in a leather bomber jacket with a scarf wrapped around his neck, the ends tucked against his chest. She had the hood of her sweater hanging over her jacket collar to protect her neck and block any drafts.

She was warm enough, but the steam coming from

the mugs on the table was a welcoming sight. "I didn't expect this."

Aaron pulled out her chair. "It's a prelude to an apology. The real apology is going to be much nicer with hot food in a restaurant, but I had to do something now."

"How is this an apology?"

"It is the scene of two crimes. At least the ignition spot."

"The arson! Have you found whoever did it?"

"We did. It took all weekend, but we tracked down the ones who got away from the parties. Ryan Dempsey was not entirely forthcoming about who was in attendance. Joseph Piney Junior's kids realized that nobody was coming here anymore, so they started using it for weekend parties while they were at college. Gerald had no idea. Joe the third invited some friends to the last one. They had a few beers, decided it was too cold, and decided to move the barbecue inside. Then things got out of hand." Aaron had gone into Minneapolis to personally interview the family. "I guess the grandson confessed to his parents, which was one of the reasons they were dodging my calls. Caleb Quentin is in the clear for everything."

"That's good to hear. He's a good kid."

"He is." Aaron took a deep breath, then stood even taller. He stared her straight in the eye. "What was criminal was the way I behaved. I'm sorry, Brooke. For accusing you of hiding information from me when you were trying to figure out what to do with some shocking news. For saying you didn't respect my job when I was the one who forgot where the line was between my career and my personal life. For getting mad that you were just being a good person trying to help Caleb when I wasn't able to help. I'm...I'm just really sorry."

Brooke was speechless. She hadn't expected anything like this. This was everything she'd said to him, but she thought he'd brushed it all off. It sounded like he'd listened to every word. "Thank you, Aaron. That means a lot."

"Not as much as you mean to me. You were right. My cop-button is stuck on the on position. I had Poppy look up the last time I took any real time off. She had to go back three summers to find a week of vacation days in a row. I have to remember how to take off the uniform again."

"You're too good a sheriff to get burned out, Aaron. The town needs you, but it needs you healthy and able to do your job."

"That's what Mac said too. So did Gene Wyatt."

"So, what are you going to do?" This was the most frustrating thing about being an adult. Knowing what had to be done, but not being able to do it for somebody else. She hoped Aaron would at least let her help."

"To start with, after Halloween, I've booked a week off. I was already planning to take a day to do a campus tour of the Woodlands Trades Institute with Trevor. Now I'm going to take a couple days and go hunting with Roy."

Traipsing through the bush with a rifle didn't sound like a relaxing day to her, but Aaron was smiling at the thought of it. "You sound like you're looking forward to it."

"I haven't gone out in a couple of years. Then I'm going to stop hogging all the on-call nights and spread them equally throughout the department. That way I can have more time to spend with this incredible, kind, helpful, beautiful woman I know. If she'll forgive me for being a jerk."

She couldn't stand fast enough to hug the man in front of her. "Yes, I forgive you for being a gigantic jerk."

"A gigantic one, huh?"

"You pretty much said I was an accessory after the fact to a break-and-enter."

"Gigantic works." He huffed a small laugh. "We need to get you to stop using television crime-show vocabulary."

"Maybe you could teach me the real words. After you're back from vacation."

"It's a deal."

When he hooked his finger under her chin and tilted her face for a kiss, Brooke closed her eyes and enjoyed the warmth of his lips on hers. "Now that's an apology," she said once he let her go.

"Tell me I didn't ruin what we were building," he whispered. "I was halfway in love with you at the corn maze and what I was feeling was growing by the day until I took a torch to it. Please say you still feel the same way."

"You rocked me pretty badly, Aaron. I understand why you were mad, but that didn't make you right. And my cape-wearing days aren't coming to an end anytime soon. I'm still going to fight for people who deserve it. Are you going to be able to deal with that as part of the whole awesome Brooke package?" That was her big worry. She knew he had a good heart, and she could forgive his frustration in a bad situation, but it wasn't something she was willing to tolerate as part of their potential future life together.

"I can. I promise," he said. "And if I can't be both your man and the town's sheriff, I'll step back and let one of my deputies deal with the legal situation while I support you. Because I'll support you as much as I love you, Brooke."

"I love you, too, Aaron."

He kissed her again, and the entire world disappeared. When they broke apart, the world erupted into a joyous chorus of fall. Leaves rustled in the wind, and a pair of sparrows in the pine tree by the road burst into song.

Aaron pulled out her chair again, and once she was seated, he topped up her coffee before sitting down himself. "What have I missed since I've been Cop Aaron twenty-four hours a day for the last week? Boyfriend Aaron needs to catch up."

"I had my midterm on Monday," Brooke told him.

He flinched. "I didn't even call to wish you luck."

"You'd wished me luck before the fire. I used that. Now I'm waiting on my results."

"I'll bet you aced it."

She crossed her fingers. "I hope so."

"What else is going on?"

Brooke had missed this. Filling in each other about their days, the big stuff and the mundane. Having someone to share the ups and the downs with. "The school board refused to address the issue of gender bias in their dress code at their last meeting. Two of the members acknowledge Jordan's op-ed piece that the parking space allocation system was unfair, so they're opening that up for public discussion next month."

"That sounds like it'll be a good time."

"My baby girl will have a portfolio that will knock the socks off any journalism school admission panel, that's for sure." For the last week, Jordan had been putting together admission packages. She'd spent hours with her father over video conferences discussing themes for her entrance essay. Jordan planned to have them all in the mail by the end of the month. She was hoping for conditional acceptance letters for Christmas. "How about you?"

"Sadly, I already told you most of my news. A campus tour with Trevor. Hunting with Roy. If it were summer, I could take a few days and go camping. Or if it was winter, I could take a snowmobiling trip. I guess I'll have to stay home and watch baseball playoffs."

After seeing his collection of ball caps, Brooke recognized his sarcasm. "Poor baby."

"I know, right?" He grinned, and there was a hint of real enthusiasm behind it. Mostly Aaron still looked tired. She been telling him he needed a break for weeks, but now she saw that she'd underestimated the situation. He needed a rest. He wasn't approaching burnout; the candle he was burning at both ends was already flickering.

"I have a little good news, too," she said. "Caleb has moved into his new studio apartment a few days early. He cleaned it and has been sleeping on the floor in a sleeping bag while he and Lucy have been painting. Once they're done, we're going to try to get him some furniture and housewares to help set him up. Right now, he's out of his car and has a place to shower and cook meals. That's good."

"That's huge." It was nice that something he'd investigated had ended without criminal charges. "We have three old sofas in the basement. Since the only people ever down there are Trevor and his friends, I'll bet he'd be willing to give one up. If Caleb will accept a gift from me."

"You won't know until you ask." The teenager had accepted a lot of charity in the last few days. It was hard on the ego to acknowledge that you needed that much help. On the other hand, Caleb seemed to have a practical head on his shoulders, and a sofa was a sofa. Practically every teenager in the country had hand-me-down furniture in their first apartment.

"Maybe I can ask him over for pizza on Friday night. Or ask Trevor too. I want Caleb to know he's still welcome."

"I'll leave that for you boys to figure out." Aaron wasn't the only one who'd come to some personal realizations. Brooke, reluctantly, had recently acknowledged that she wasn't the world's best juggler. Between Jordan, her job at the Dew Drop Inn, her classes, and Aaron, her schedule was full to bursting. Running the Jackson Corn Maze fundraiser had pushed her over the edge; it had taken two weeks to make up the study time she'd missed. She couldn't work on any more of Jordan's senior fundraisers and fulfill her regular volunteer commitments while she was going back to school. She'd had to turn down a shift at the food bank because she still needed to sleep. Brooke felt like she should be doing more, but there wasn't any way to create more hours in the day. Aaron was going to have to fix his history with Caleb on his own.

"When you get your marks back, I'd like to take you out to celebrate," Aaron said. "It's been a while since we've had a nice date night. I'll make sure to send everybody to whoever is on duty that night, which definitely won't be me."

It wasn't graceful, but Brooke managed to stand and lean over the card table to kiss him again. "That sounds perfect."

CHAPTER 34

THE NEXT DAY, the Dew Drop Inn was in a rush to get ready for a prospective wedding party who were coming to tour the premises. Their wedding business had tripled in the six months since Mickey Wagner had taken over. There hadn't been much time to get into wedding bookings for that summer, but next year was looking like it would be back-to-back brides. She stuck around long enough to see Mickey start the visit and overheard the guests talking about the spotless hotel. When her boss flashed her a thumbs-up behind the guests' backs as she walked out the door, Brooke left smiling.

She had to hurry. She and Aaron would only have a short time to have supper to celebrate her midterm exam grade before he had to return to patrolling on the night before Halloween. During the trick-or-treat season, Aaron told her that most of the tricks happened on the thirtieth.

Brooke took extra time getting ready. Not because she was with Aaron, which was always nice, but because she was celebrating herself tonight. She'd earned it. She thought she'd been crazy to go back to school at her age while working full-time, and she wasn't sure she'd make it. She and Jordan had to sacrifice a lot for her to chase that dream, but it was paying off.

Supper with Aaron was rushed, but still wonderful. Even in the day they'd been apart, each of them had news to share. Caleb had accepted Trevor's invitation to come over on Friday, and Aaron was planning to order pizza to celebrate Caleb's new apartment. The sofa issue was still unresolved, but Brooke assured him it was an excellent first step.

After an exceptional chicken piccata, their waiter brought out two pieces of pumpkin pie as part of the Halloween special. "I love this time of year. I'll eat pumpkin pie from the beginning of October to the end of November. I don't know who decided that we should prioritize other kinds for the rest of the year," Aaron said as he took a spoonful of the whip cream piled on top.

"It makes it more of a treat," she said.

"Speaking of treats, and hopefully not tricks, don't you have some news for me?" Aaron asked. "Did you get your grades back on your midterm exam?"

"I got them back alright." Brooke still couldn't believe it.

She took a sip of coffee, then another bite of pie.

"Are you going to tell me what you got?"

"Oh, you just asked if I got them back. Did you want to know what my grade was?"

"It's not too late to arrest you, you know," Aaron growled.

"Okay. In that case, you might be interested to know that I got..." She faked a cough, then took another sip of coffee.

"Brooke!"

"Ninety-two percent!" she crowed. "The second-highest score in the class."

"I'm dating a genius!"

"I know." She didn't try to hide her pride. She'd worked hard for that grade. "But it gets better. My professor contacted me this morning. She said that, between my marks on my introductory accounting course over the summer and my first assignment and my midterm, I might be able to qualify for a scholarship for next semester if I maintain my grades."

"That's fantastic!" Aaron raised his water glass. "Congratulations twice to my brilliant girlfriend. I know you can get that scholarship."

"Thank you." She reached across the table to grab his hand and give it a squeeze. "I think I scared Jordan with my squeal when I got that call. It could cover the next two courses in my program, plus all my books."

"How do you feel about depreciation rates now?"

"They're my favorite, tied with mortgage interest calculations. I love depreciation. Next is capital gains taxation. I can't wait!" She surprised herself, because she meant it. Despite all the work and hours that she spent studying, she did actually enjoy the subject. Most people wouldn't find numbers that fascinating, but they made sense for her.

"You have no idea how much I'm learning about accounting just by being with you," Aaron said. His words were joking, but his tone was serious. "How important it is for debits and credits and pros and cons to balance. How to decide if paying a penalty is worth the price in the long run." He hadn't let go of her fingers, and now he covered it with his other hand, holding her in a warm cocoon. "Figuring out the true cost of something."

"And discovering that some things are truly priceless," she added quietly.

"I love you, Brooke. I don't care that we're in the middle of pie. I'm going to kiss you now," he announced.

He dragged his tie through the whipped cream, and Brooke knocked her fork to the floor, but the kiss was totally worth it. It said everything about what they'd been through and where they were going. And now the whole town knew it. There was only one problem: if his kisses got any better, Brooke thought she might spontaneously combust.

Aaron sat down again wearing a completely satisfied grin. He still hadn't let go of her hand. Until he suddenly dropped it, then pointed into the middle of the restaurant. "Neil Dempsey, if you are coming over her to complain about something, don't. Call the station to make your report. Because if you say anything to me tonight, I'm going to arrest you on first-degree murder charges for killing my excellent mood."

The scowling man turned on his heel and stalked out of the dining room, followed by the amused chuckles of other patrons.

Aaron grabbed her hand again. "Now where was I?"

"Before you told me you loved me, you were complimenting me for being a brilliant student," Brooke prompted.

"Right. You're a genius. A star scholar."

"Do go on."

"A shining example of a bookkeeping wunderkind," he continued. "You are a little obsessed with haunted cornfields, though."

She shrugged, then winked at him. "Nobody's perfect. But I'm close."

CHAPTER 35

"TRICK OR TREAT!" Brooke heard the call echo down the street and up the stairwell, where Lucy Callahan had staked out a step near the front door and was handing out candy to all the little boos and ghouls who arrived in costume to celebrate the spookiest night of the year. Brooke pulled on thick wool socks, zipped her hoodie over her flannel shirt, and headed downstairs to keep her friend company.

It was unseasonably cold for the last day of October. Any jack-o'-lanterns left outside wouldn't make it through to morning without frost damage. The weather channel was already predicting a slight chance of overnight snow. The kids were making the most of this last day of October.

"Grab a bowl of candy and join me," Lucy said in greeting. "We have tons, so give it out by the handful."

Brooke checked out the offered pail of goodies. Inside was a hodgepodge of gums, jelly candies, and mini-candy bars. "What? No toothbrushes? No sugar-free snacks?"

"You don't have to help with that attitude."

"I'm kidding. It's practically perfect."

"Practically?" Lucy asked.

"No licorice."

"That's it. Back to your apartment, young lady, until you can behave yourself."

"The chocolate will do."

Lucy tossed her a mini-bar, and they settled in for the next wave.

The trick or treaters travelled in packs, descending on houses with the porch lights on like ravenous candy-beasts. Princesses and superheroes were by far the costumes of choice, but Brooke's favorite of the elementary school crowd was a short-haired kid in an oversized yellow sweater with a black zigzag stripe on it, and his sister in a blue dress and black wig, carrying a football. Snoopy was a toddler who was passed out in a stroller on the sidewalk, his blackened nose tilted up and the floppy ears on his hat askew. She had no problem putting a handful of candy into his little basket, even though he wasn't awake to say thank you.

"Look! Isn't Owen's son darling?" Lucy whispered, as a familiar masked criminal held hands with a little Spidey who was racing up the sidewalk.

"Trick or candy!" the tiny superhero shouted.

Owen Daye slapped his hand over his face. "Richie, we discussed this."

"Close enough," Brooke announced as she gave the boy a handful of chocolate bars. "Be sure to share some with your daddy, okay?"

"Okay!"

A police cruiser pulled to the curb. "Hey, look, Spidey. Here's the police. Do you want Sheriff Gillespie to take this robber off your hands?"

"No, he's my dad. It's just pretend."

Brooke couldn't help herself. She elbowed Lucy in the ribs. "Yeah, it's just pretend."

"I forgot. Have a happy Halloween, Spidey."

"Do you happen to know if By the Cup is open tonight? I promised Pops I'd bring him home something warm since he got stuck with candy duty on the front porch," Owen said, scratching at his blond hair beneath his mask.

"I think Rachel's staying open till nine o'clock tonight. I assume your webslinger will be in bed long before then if you can make a caffeine run later."

"My dad can watch him," Owen said. "Do you know if Miss Best herself will be working tonight? She doesn't seem to like me much."

"I thought that Rachel liked everybody," Brooke said in surprise.

"I must be the exception to that rule. We keep running into each other at antique shows in the area, but all I get is the cold shoulder," Owen said. "I'll brave the chill, though. Pops said she has the best coffee north of Minneapolis."

"Tell her that," Lucy suggested. "Maybe she'll warm up to you."

"I can hope," Owen said.

"Dad, we have to go get more candy. Bye!" Richie yelled.

Owen waved as his son dragged him away, saluting the sheriff as they passed on the sidewalk. "Sorry about the shouting. He only has one volume."

Brooke laughed. "I remember those days. Have fun tonight, Owen."

It was Lucy's turn to elbow her. "Take Aaron for a walk around the block. I've got the door."

Brooke met Aaron on the sidewalk. He took her hand and quickly pulled her around the corner of the building, where he gave her a toe-tingling kiss. "Happy Halloween to you, too," she said.

"That was a thank you for the treats you've left for me around town."

"How did you figure it out it was me?" she asked.

"I am a trained investigator."

She knew Aaron was going to have a busy night, with calls for everything from accidents to hauntings, so she'd decided to make it worth his while. With a little help from Poppy Zimmer, she already knew some of his predetermined stops. Brooke guessed at a couple of others. Then she spent an hour after work running around, dropping off care packages for run-off-their-feet sheriffs. They weren't much: usually a baggie with two or three gummy candy packages or mini-chocolate bars tied with a ribbon and a little "Happy Halloween" card from a variety of female detectives, from Miss Marple to Veronica Mars to Olivia Benson. "Are they helping?"

"They're keeping my sugar levels up tonight, which is all I can ask for. I'm going to crash hard in the morning." He looked tired, but it wasn't the bone-tired exhaustion he'd worn a few days ago. Brooke had called him every evening and checked to see if he was on call and if he was going to bed at a reasonable hour. The difference even in two days was noticeable.

"Want to have a late lunch tomorrow?" she asked. "I can swing by when I get off work."

"That sounds like a great way to kick off my vacation."

"Do you know what we could do later?"

"I'm intrigued and terrified at what you might suggest."

"Glenna Jackson is mowing down the corn maze. Do you want to go watch with me?"

Aaron laughed long and loud before he kissed her. "Sure. That sounds like a good way to say goodbye to a month filled with terrified and terrifying screaming goats, a band of roving, destructive partiers, an abandoned ramshackle shack that went up in a blaze of glory, and a confession-extracting scarecrow, although Detective Hayseed will definitely be back next year, because that guy is good."

"On the other hand, it was also a month of successfully raising funds for our children's graduation, acing some tests and assignments, remembering how to relax, helping a young man get on track, and starting a pretty decent romance," Brooke countered.

"Pretty decent? I'd say one that deserves celebrating all year round, but I'll settle for saying it was the best Halloween ever."

ABOUT THE AUTHOR

Elle Rush is a contemporary romance author from Winnipeg, Manitoba, Canada. When she's not travelling, she's hard at work writing books which are set all over the world. From Hollywood to the house next door, her heroes will make you sigh and her heroines will make you laugh out loud.

Elle has a degree in Spanish and French, barely passed German, and has flunked poetry in every language she ever studied, including English. She also has mild addictions to tea, her garden, bad sci-fi movies, and HGTV.

Keep up with her new releases by subscribing to her newsletter at **www.ellerush.com/newsletter**.

ALSO BY ELLE RUSH

SWEET CONTEMPORARY ROMANCE

<u>Holiday Beach</u>

(also available in paperback)

Shamrocks and Surprises

Pumpkins and Promises

Tinsel and Teacups

Fireworks and Frenemies

<u>North Pole Unlimited</u>

Decker and Joy

Hollis and Ivy

Nick and Eve

Rudy and Kris

Ben and Jilly

Frank and Ginger

<u>North Pole Unlimited Collections</u>

(also available in paperback)

Collection 1 - Decker & Joy, Hollis & Ivy

Collection 2 - Nick & Eve, Rudy & Kris

Collection 3 - Ben & Jilly, Frank & Ginger